From the back of the church, footsteps—like nails striking the flagstones of the aisle.

A voice, harsh and strident, breaking the hallowed silence. Heads turning, breaths intaking across the congregation.

A voice calling out.

Announcing. Denouncing...

Luca felt his head turn. Felt his gaze fall on the figure of the woman walking down the aisle. A red suit, exposing every curve of her voluptuous body. A matching pillbox hat with a black veil concealing her upper face.

A veil she threw back as she approached.

To his side he heard Tomaso give a snarl of rage, start forward.

But he himself did not move. Could not.

Could only level his eyes on her with a fury he had not known he could possess that should strike her to silence if there were any justice in the world—any decency.

But there was no justice, no decency. There was only her voice, ringing out like sacrilege. Freezing him to the very marrow of his bones.

"He *cannot* marry her!" she cried out. "I am pregnant with his child!"

Julia James lives in England and adores the peaceful verdant countryside and the wild shores of Cornwall. She also loves the Mediterranean—so rich in myth and history, with its sunbaked landscapes and olive groves, ancient ruins and azure seas. “The perfect setting for romance!” she says. “Rivaled only by the lush tropical heat of the Caribbean—palms swaying by a silver-sand beach lapped by turquoise waters... What more could lovers want?”

Books by Julia James

Harlequin Presents

Billionaire’s Mediterranean Proposal
Irresistible Bargain with the Greek
The Greek’s Duty-Bound Royal Bride
The Greek’s Penniless Cinderella
Cinderella in the Boss’s Palazzo
Cinderella’s Baby Confession
Destitute Until the Italian’s Diamond

One Night With Consequences

Heiress’s Pregnancy Scandal

Visit the Author Profile page
at Harlequin.com for more titles.

Julia James

THE COST OF CINDERELLA'S CONFESSION

ISBN-13: 978-1-335-73899-8

The Cost of Cinderella's Confession

For questions and comments about the quality of this book, please contact us at CustomerService@Harlequin.com.

Harlequin Enterprises ULC
22 Adelaide St. West, 41st Floor
Toronto, Ontario M5H 4E3, Canada
www.Harlequin.com

Printed in U.S.A.

THE COST OF CINDERELLA'S CONFESSION

For Nic—a huge thank-you!

PROLOGUE

THE MEDIEVAL CHURCH was bathed in the warm sunshine filling the *piazza* in the ancient hilltop town in central Italy. Sunshine that did not warm Ariana. Instead, only cold filled her. Cold that almost had her shivering. Or something did.

Fear.

Fear of what she was about to do—what she had to nerve herself to do…steel herself to do.

Face set, hidden from view by the little veil that dipped from the deliberately stylish and very expensive hat, which went with the equally stylish and expensive tightly cinched suit curving over her shapely figure, she walked up to the arched entrance of the church, invitation at the ready.

The service had already started, and the choir were singing an anthem as she slipped unobtrusively into a seat at the back. She sat down, feeling sick with nerves, wishing with all her being that she could just bolt and run. But she *had* to do this.

She bowed her head, as if in prayer, but actually to avoid looking at the well-dressed congregation…or the figures by the altar rail. Another rush of fearfulness assailed her at the enormity of what she was about to do.

But there's no other way—none!

The anthem finished, there was a rustling among the congregation, and then the priest—a high-ranking cleric, as befitted so grand a society wedding—began to intone the words of the ceremony.

A dizziness filled Ariana's head, and her heart was hammering. She had to time this right—totally and absolutely right—to the very moment.

The dreaded moment.

The dreadful moment…

And then it came. The words that had never received a response at any wedding she'd been to. But today, right now, they would. They must…

There's no other way—however much I long with all my being not to do this!

She heard the priest say the words—her cue, her signal. Heard the dutiful pause that followed. Heard herself stand, step into the wide aisle. She started to walk forward, every step compelled from her by a strength of will to overcome her repugnance at what she was doing. What she was about to do.

She started to speak, forcing the words out through her constricted throat. The words she *had* to say, falling like a sacrilege across the sacrament of holy matrimony. Words to halt it in its tracks.

'*Yes!* I have an objection! And I will not hold my peace! This marriage cannot take place!'

She saw heads turn, heard the collective gasp of shock from the congregation as they stared at her, striding down the aisle on high heels that struck like nails on the flagstones, towards the two figures by the altar rail.

The bride, a slender column in white, her face invisible beneath a long lace veil, did not move. But the groom did. Ariana's fixed gaze saw him turn. Slowly, like a jaguar that had just heard something behind him move. Something that might be prey—or a fellow predator.

The cold inside her froze instantly to solid ice as his gaze came to rest on her. It was as if liquid nitrogen had just been poured down her throat. She felt her senses sway, and with every instinct in her body she wanted to halt and turn…and flee…

But she would not. *Could* not. She had to do this. Had to play it to the very end.

His eyes, like a basilisk, watched her approach. They were all that she could see.

Not the man who had given away the bride, now starting forward with an oath, nor the bride herself, still not turning, motionless like a statue. Let alone the best man, the half-dozen bridesmaids, flower girls and page boys all staring open-mouthed at her approach.

Not even the priest stepping forward now, his expression half concerned, because her interruption must, in light of his professional duty, be attended to, and half holding the collective outrage she could feel coming at her in waves from the congregation at her stupendous, scandalous social *faux pas* in doing what she was so appallingly doing.

The priest opened his mouth to speak, to demand the reason for her outburst, but she pre-empted him. She stopped dead, some way still from the altar rail and the front row of pews, and threw back her short veil.

And *then* she saw the basilisk eyes change.

Saw recognition.

For a second, a micron of time so short it almost ceased to exist, she saw something flare in the obsidian eyes. A black flame…

Then it was gone. Now in his eyes there was only a blade so sharp she could feel it cutting the flesh from her bones.

He started forward, but she was already speaking. Her voice a clarion, heard by all present. Heard by the motionless bride, her back still turned to her. Heard by the groom, with tension in every line of his tall, lean body, every plane of his hard, stark face. In the sculpted mouth now whipped to a narrow line.

She pointed her hand as she spoke, praying that it was not trembling. An accusing hand. Directed at the groom. The man whose wedding she had to stop. Right now.

'He *cannot* marry her!' she cried out. 'I am pregnant with his child!'

CHAPTER ONE

Three months earlier...

ARIANA GLANCED AT her reflection in the mirror in the ladies' room of the uptown, upmarket Manhattan hotel, her peat-coloured eyes, a legacy of her father, deepened by eyeshadow and mascara, her generous mouth lustrous with lipstick.

Her grandfather would say she looked like a harlot, but she didn't care—he always thought badly of her. Nothing she could do pleased him. Even when she tried to dress demurely he still disparaged her. She was too tall, too full-figured, too curvaceous, too everything. And, worst of all, far, far too outspoken. Always drawing attention to herself in entirely the wrong way.

Unlike her cousin Mia.

It was Mia who was the granddaughter he approved of. Mia, so petite, so slender, with her long fair hair and angelic features. Mia, so gentle and sweet-natured. Quietly spoken, diffident—meek, docile and shy. Just as a woman should be.

That was their grandfather's opinion, and he did not balk at holding forth about it.

Ariana had heard it all her life, even as a child, and certainly once she became a teenager. She should be inured to it, but it could still sting—even now.

Well, not tonight! Tonight she was four thousand miles away from her grandfather's grand *palazzo* in Umbria and she was going to enjoy herself. She'd just completed the refurbishment of her mother's new house in Florida, bought with her latest husband—number five, as Ariana had totted it up—and she'd flown to New York to catch up with her other American clients, including her hostess tonight: wealthy socialite Marnie van Huren, a friend of Ariana's mother, who was bubbly, sociable—and matchmaking.

'Come to my party, honey, and get yourself a nice man! You career girls are always too busy for romance!'

Ariana had smiled but said nothing. She focussed on her career for a reason—and it wasn't to compensate for a lack of romance in her life. It was to escape her grandfather's financial control.

It was a control that was not just financial, but emotional as well—a control he'd always sought to exert over his family. He'd done it with her uncle, Mia's father, who to his dying day had never stepped out of line any more than his daughter—sweet, docile Mia—did now. That hideous day Ariana's uncle and aunt had been killed in a car crash, when Mia was seven and she was nine. The tragedy had scarred them all, making her grandfather's stifling tyranny even more suffocating. He'd become determined to make Ariana like gentle Mia, wanting to chain his granddaughters to his side, not wanting them to have a cent that had not been bestowed upon them by himself even once they'd grown up.

Ariana had vowed never to be dependent, never to let her grandfather curb and constrain her as he did her timid, gentle cousin Mia. Nor to react to that crushing control in the way her own mother had. She had eloped at nineteen with a good-looking penniless wastrel who had soon abandoned her, freshly married and pregnant, in exchange for being bought off by an irate father-in-law, never to be seen again. Least of all by his daughter Ariana.

A succession of marriages interspersed with affairs had followed for her mother, all disapproved of by Ariana's grandfather, but fortunately always to wealthy men.

Ariana had no intention of copying her mother's solution to her grandfather's tyranny. She would never be dependent on a man's largesse, whoever that man was. She would make her own money, using her own talents.

It hadn't proved easy, and her precarious efforts to succeed in the overcrowded world of interior design were yet another source of contemptuous disapproval by her grandfather—yet another reason to condemn her. But she'd been dogged in her persistence and her determination, and now, at twenty-seven, she felt she could call herself a success.

It wasn't, of course, a success that earned her grandfather's approval—nothing could do that—but it earned her enough money to live a comfortably affluent life. The downside was that it was a life dedicated to her career. Though she dated from time to time, it was never a priority for her. Romance, for now, came a very poor second.

But when she finally had time for romance she would make sure it was the real thing. Permanent. She would not be like her mother, flitting from man to man, husband to husband. No, for her it would be different. One man, one love, one life—together.

One day I'll meet him! The man I'll make my life with—who will mean everything to me. The one man in the world who'll set me alight like a flame, to burn for him all my life!

It would happen one day—and in the meantime there was work and, like tonight, socialising.

She glanced at her reflection again. The figure-hugging cocktail dress showed her generous curves in a way that would have had her grandfather choking. Defiantly, she gave a toss of her head, sending rich brunette waves rippling over her shoulders as, with a final glance, she sashayed out on her five-inch heels and went to party.

Luca Farnese stood at the side of the crowded function room, which was noisy with chatter and the clink of glasses and bejewelled bracelets, and surveyed the scene. He would not be staying long at this high-society Manhattan shindig, only long enough to have the conversation he wanted with his host, and then he'd escape.

Even though he knew, without vanity, that he was being eyed up, courtesy of his darkly good-looking Italian features, his six-foot height and lean, fit body, he had no desire for any dalliance tonight. Or ever. He had already found the woman of his dreams—and she was all he had ever sought in the woman he would make his life with.

A memory of her across the ocean, waiting for him to return and declare himself to her, played in his head, conjuring up her angelical beauty, her fair hair, luminous blue eyes, her tender mouth and her soft, melodious voice. She hadn't said a great deal, had only hidden her doe-like gaze beneath demure lashes, but from the moment he'd met her—only a handful of weeks ago—he'd been captivated by her. The gentle sweetness of her nature had shone through, and the air of quietness about her had been serene and tranquil. What he had always dreamt of—longed for.

And he knew why.

Bitterly so.

Memory slid back down the years, the decades, and his expression tightened in painful recollection. Raised voices, doors slamming. His father's voice, pleading and placatory, his mother's angry and denouncing, vitriolic in its complaint and criticism, unstoppable in the full flow of her histrionics. Then a final slamming of a door and silence. Oppressive, echoing silence.

Himself as a young boy, clutching the landing banisters with clammy hands, his expression strained and anxious. Then going back to his bedroom with a heavy, forlorn tread, his insides knotted up, his heart thumping as he climbed back into bed. But not to sleep. To stare tensely up at the ceiling, hands clenched either side of his stiff body, trying to block out the echoes of the shouting and cursing.

He'd wished his mother wasn't always quarrelling with his father, yelling at him, storming out, making scenes wherever she was, in front of everyone, even in front of complete strangers, not giving a damn that people were looking, not caring about her son's mortification, her husband's cringing embarrassment. However badly his mother behaved, his father seemed to be in thrall to her, letting her endlessly get away with her outbursts.

As a boy he'd been unable to understand why—but as he became a teenager, and then a man, he'd come to understand the power his mother had over his father. The power of her blatant sexuality that his hapless father had never been able to resist.

Rejection of his father's endless surrender to his wife's sensual allure had brought Luca to a steely resolve for himself. His own marriage would be nothing like his tormented parents'. Never would he be in sexual thrall to a woman as his father had been, and nor would his wife be like his demanding, self-absorbed mother, who'd cared nothing for her hapless husband and her neglected son.

No, the woman he would fall in love with—his ideal since his teenage years—would be the very opposite. Quiet and gentle, sweet-natured and loving, never raising her voice to anyone. And all he'd want would be her happiness, as he bestowed upon her his devotion and his wealth.

Wealth he had made for himself, in the cut-throat world of high finance. Wealth of which he was now in continued pursuit—and he needled his glance through the guests, looking for fellow financier Charles van Huren, whom he had arranged to meet here.

Charles's business schedule was as non-stop as his own, and as Luca was flying back to Italy the next morning it meant that tonight, albeit at Charles's wife's birthday party, was the only opportunity they would have to discuss the joint business investment they were contemplating.

He levered himself away from the wall, intent on finding his host in the crowd. He gave a cursory glance into the room opening off to his left, from which throbbing dance music was emanating. As he did so, someone caught his eye.

A woman…dancing on her own.

Ariana could feel the slow, heavy beat of the music, the old, familiar number echoing in her pulse as she moved to it, murmuring the well-worn lyrics of the track with a nostalgic half-smile playing on her lips.

Without conscious volition she moved on to the floor, started to dance, not caring that she had no one to dance with, wanting only to feel the slug of the music, to give herself to it, her feet moving indolently, arms twining, serpentine, winding in and out of the intoxicating melody.

Feeling the luxuriant tresses of her hair loosened from their customary businesslike confines and moving across her shoulders like a silky cloud, she dipped her head, hair swaying, heartrate synching with the heavy music. Losing all sense of time, she was becoming one with the music, primitive, primeval, caught in its low, seductive beat.

Then the music ended, and lights flared in a blaze. She looked up, throwing her head back, catching her breath as her eyes focussed.

Straight into the watching gaze of a man standing at the edge of the dance floor, looking straight at her.

Luca stood immobile, his gaze fixed. Why the hell had he stopped as he had?

It was a pointless question to ask himself. He knew exactly why.

The woman was tall, her height accentuated by heels that threw her lush body, tightly sheathed in a dark red dress, into lusher curves yet, lengthening her slender legs. Her long, loose hair cascaded down her back, framing a face as breathtaking as her body, with huge dark eyes and a curving, wanton mouth…

The woman who had just stopped dancing would have drawn the eye of a saint.

And he was no saint…

He felt his body quicken with incipient arousal. He crushed it down. He wasn't in the market for an encounter of any kind. Not any longer. And certainly not with a woman like the one he was staring at.

Before, when he'd wanted…needed…a woman he'd picked carefully. Very carefully. Someone to dine with, talk with—politics, business, finance—and take to bed. High-flying women, nearly always working in the same field as himself, with whom it was therefore easy to converse. Sleek, svelte women who wore an evening dress as if it were a business suit, with short, smooth, styled hair and discreet, immaculate make-up. Beautiful women, obviously, but women who controlled their lives as rigorously as he did his own.

The woman he'd just been watching had not been controlling her life at all. She'd let the music control it. She had melded her body with it. Arms moving sinuously, body swaying, head bowed, lost to the world…

A world she had suddenly returned to as the music had stopped and her body had stilled.

For a second her eyes, dark and huge and smoky, lifted to his, looked right at him. Then, abruptly, she was turning away, raising her hands as she did so to lift the heavy tresses of lush dark hair as if to cool her neck. It was a very natural gesture, and a sensual one…

Luca's gaze narrowed slightly. The woman's movement had lifted her breasts, which now strained against the tight material of her dress, emphasising her generous cleavage. Again, against his will, he felt his body react…

Anger stabbed. This was way out of order.

Forcing his muscles to obey him, he moved sharply away. Across the main function room he saw Charles van Huren, finally finished with his duties as host, and made eye contact. Receiving an acknowledging nod in return, he headed forward, and moments later both men had disappeared into a deserted room and settled down to their business discussion, in brisk, time-efficient tones.

All thoughts of the lushly curved brunette with her smoky eyes, sensuous dancing and mane of wild hair, were forcibly banished.

* * *

Ariana let her hair fall again, heavy on her shoulders, and as if she were following through with the gesture twisted her head towards the entrance to the dance floor. She exhaled, relief filling her. He was gone.

That moment, brief as a casual glance, had been anything but casual. Her gaze had collided with his like a physical clash, and she knew with a sudden pulse in her veins that had nothing to do with the throbbing music that it had been fastened on her. Watching her dance.

Watching *her.*

With an intensity that had felt like a spear right through her.

Instinctively she'd swivelled away from him. She was used to men looking her over. But never a man like that…

A hollow formed in her stomach as she made her way to the edge of the dance floor, seeking, suddenly, the support of a wall to lean against. His face, so briefly glimpsed, burned in her vision.

Aquiline, high cheekbones, ludicrously good looking. And eyes like obsidian…cutting right into her.

She drew a sharp intake of breath, banishing the image, glad he'd disappeared. She wasn't here for a pick-up.

Done with dancing, she headed back into the main function room, ready to mingle and relax. Some forty minutes later she was doing just that, chatting to a middle-aged couple, acquaintances of her mother, when they were joined by a friend of theirs who was, as she disclosed to Ariana on being introduced to her, very bored with the current décor in her uptown apartment. Ariana gave her her card, and then, tactfully pressing no further, slipped away, helping herself to a glass of champagne just as Marnie sailed up to her.

'Ariana, I need you to help me out! One of my guests is trying to escape!'

Ariana felt her arm taken, and was inexorably borne away by her exuberant hostess. They were heading, Ariana saw, to Marnie's husband, who was talking to a man with his back to them. She got only a moment's warning, and then she and Marnie were upon them.

The man turned.

For the second time that evening it came. That searing gaze that had lasered her while she was dancing.

Ariana felt her breath catch, her stomach muscles clench, and immediately, out of some atavistic instinct, schooled her features into unbetraying immobility. Dimly, she heard Marnie throw some arch remark at her husband about not talking business at her birthday party, and then she was turning to Ariana.

'Tell your compatriot he can't possibly leave yet!' she gushed.

'Compatriot?' Ariana heard her own voice echo.

She was conscious that she was glad to look at Marnie, and not at the man beside Charles van Huren.

'Italian—like you,' Marnie confirmed.

Wondering vaguely if it were possible that the man who had been talking to Charles van Huren might have imperfect English, Ariana felt obliged to respond to her hostess's imprecation.

'Signora van Huren implores you to enjoy the evening

of her birthday party with her most sincere wishes,' she ventured cautiously, in Italian.

It was a strain to look directly at the man, whoever he was, but she did it all the same. And as she said her piece something flickered at the back of those darker-than-dark eyes. She didn't know what—only that she found it disturbing.

But then she found everything about him disturbing. Up close like this, the impact he had made on her when she'd realised he'd been watching her dance was increased tenfold. He towered over her, even in her high heels, with his lean, taut body, and his hard-planed features once again made her breath catch.

The chiselled mouth gave a sardonic twist. 'Thank you for the translation, but I got it the first time around,' he said, in perfect, only slightly accented American-English. His voice was deep, and very dry.

Marnie gave a trill of laughter, and her husband shook his head resignedly. 'Honey, Luca only dropped by at my request. We had some business to discuss. He needs to get away now.'

His wife threw up her hands in protest. 'No, no, no! I won't have it! He's here now and I won't let him leave!'

She seized up a glass of champagne from a nearby waiter and thrust it at her unwilling guest. He took it, Ariana could see, with obvious reluctance. As he did so, she made to slip away. It was apparent her fluent command of Italian was entirely unnecessary.

But a diamond braceleted hand fastened around her wrist. 'Uh-uh!' countermanded her hostess. 'Not before I've properly introduced you!'

Ariana squirmed inwardly, but to no avail. It had suddenly dawned on her, with excruciating embarrassment, what Marnie van Huren was doing. Setting her up.

Well, she would not be rude, but she schooled her features to an expression of complete impassivity as Marnie happily burbled on, exchanging their names with each of them.

'Ms Killane…' The deep, dark voice sounded her name briefly. Inexpressively.

She gave an even briefer nod of acknowledgement, not troubling herself to echo his name in return.

Her hostess beamed all the same. 'Well, now the introductions are over I must circulate! Charles!'

She released Ariana's wrist and bore her husband off, leaving Ariana standing there like a lemon, the glass of champagne in her hand.

She gave a tightly controlled smile. 'So nice to have met you, Mr Farnese. Do please excuse me,' she murmured in deliberate English, her tone as inexpressive as his, and turned away.

She would not be complicit in her hostess's embarrassing matchmaking. Nor would she, even more excruciatingly, give the damn man any idea that she was complicit. Not waiting for a response, she threaded her way across the room, chatting animatedly with anyone she knew, even if only slightly.

She was done with the party, she realised. If Marnie van Huren was set on pairing her off, she didn't want to spend the evening avoiding her hostess's efforts. She set down her champagne, dived into the restroom, then went to the cloakroom to get her fake fur jacket and make her getaway.

She stepped out into the upper floor lobby, beyond the function rooms, and headed for the elevator.

Then stopped dead.

Luca Farnese, tall, dark, devastatingly good-looking and with those obsidian eyes that could cut like black lasers, had beaten her to it.

There was nothing else for it. She either had to bottle it, and scurry back to the party, or else hold her nerve and make her escape as she'd planned.

She opted for the latter. Head high, she stalked to the elevator.

Luca Farnese watched her approach. His face was unreadable, completely masked. Did the man think she was chasing after him? She didn't care. Because she wasn't. He could think what he liked—it didn't bother her.

Bestowing upon him only the curtest of nods of acknowledgement, she stepped gratefully into the car as the elevator doors slid open. He followed her in.

'Lobby?' he enquired.

The dark, deep voice still had that sardonic tone to it, and Ariana knew exactly why.

'Please,' she said briefly.

He jabbed with a long finger and the doors sliced shut. The car descended. It seemed to leave Ariana's stomach somewhere on the function room floor as it did so. Or something did.

She did not look at her fellow passenger, staring fixedly ahead. As the doors sliced open again he stood aside, letting her emerge first. She stalked across the marble lobby towards the hotel's revolving doors. Out on the pavement the air was chilly, and she clutched her jacket around her. A doorman beckoned a taxi for her, opening the passenger door as Ariana stepped forward.

A voice sounded behind her. Deep and speaking Italian.

'Have dinner with me,' said Luca Farnese.

CHAPTER TWO

THE RESTAURANT WAS QUIET, and Luca liked it that way, it was why he patronised it when he was in New York. As the waiter bestowed menus upon them he found his thoughts flickering like a faulty circuit.

Why the hell had he gone and done this? It didn't make logical sense. He should have headed back to his hotel, dined in his suite and had an early night before his flight to Milan the next day. Then at the weekend he'd be heading south, into the heart of Italy, to Umbria. To change his life for ever.

With a woman as unlike the one he'd brought here as it was possible to be.

The faulty circuit shorted out. His gaze lifted from the menu to the lush brunette Charles's wife had so blatantly introduced him to. He'd been as dismissive about the introduction as civility permitted, and yet, when she had been similarly dismissive of him, he had been illogically put out. Was that why he'd made his impulsive dinner invitation to her?

His dark eyes rested on her now, as still he questioned himself. Her focus was entirely on the menu, and it allowed his gaze to linger. That fabulous hair, a wanton cloud around her shoulders, long and luxuriant, those huge, long-lashed smoky eyes, the full, wide mouth, lush with deep red lipstick to match the burgundy of her dress pulled tight across her generous breasts.

Sensuous, sensual… He'd known it from the moment he'd watched her dance. Unable to *not* watch her… And yet—he frowned inwardly—she was totally different from the kind of women he had affairs with—the sleek, corporate executive types, with sharp hair and sharp minds and slim, gym-fit bodies.

This woman, seated opposite him now, couldn't be more different. And not just from the style of women he was used to. In his head flickered a projected image of the woman waiting for him in Italy—half a world away. Angelically fair, celestial blue eyes…

The image flickered again and cut out. Gone. As if she no longer existed. At least for now.

Only the woman sitting opposite him remained, dominating his vision, his senses, his consciousness, blocking out everything else. Every*one* else.

Why? Why am I doing this when it is not what I planned at all? And why this woman?

The questions speared his head, seeking an answer from his keenly honed, coolly rational brain. Finding none.

He snapped his mind away from what he was doing and why he was doing it, forcibly returning his attention to his choice for dinner.

'Have you decided?' He closed his menu, setting it down on the linen tablecloth and looking across at her.

Ariana Killane. Her name hung in the space between them. Italian and Irish. A potent combination. He'd asked her about it in the taxi here. It had seemed like a neutral subject to begin their evening together.

'Killane? And yet you speak perfect Italian?' he'd thrown at her questioningly.

'Irish father. Italian mother,' had come the reply.

She hadn't looked at him, hadn't quite met his eyes across the narrow space in the cab.

Yet he knew she was as burningly aware of him as he was of her—it radiated from her. Just as it had when she'd so briefly met his fixated gaze when she'd stopped dancing, and when she'd immediately walked off after Charles's wife's blatant introduction, and when she'd stalked out of the elevator across the lobby. He felt it now, in the way she still didn't meet his eyes as she answered his question in a faux casual manner.

'I'll be predictable, I think…'

Luca heard her response to his question and was glad to take his thoughts away from where it was inconvenient for them to go.

'The *tournedos rossini.*'

He gave a nod. 'Good choice. It's mine too.'

For a moment her choice of such a rich dish surprised him. Then, his eyes going to her generous figure, he realised it did not. This was no stick-thin *fashionista.* This was a woman nature had bountifully endowed with a sensual appeal and a body to match.

He beckoned the waiter, watched the sommelier coming over too. After both had been despatched, he let his eyes rest on the woman he'd invited, without any logic or sense, to have dinner with him.

And whatever came after.

Ariana reached for her wine glass. She felt she needed it. What in God's name did she think she was doing? She'd let this man—a complete stranger but for his name—commandeer her taxi and bring her here to this oh-so-discreetly quiet French restaurant.

Beside the taxi she'd turned, astonished at his invitation, given that he'd clearly not even wanted to be introduced to her and that she'd stalked away from him. So what had changed his mind? Or hers?

I wasn't looking for this...

Yet it had happened.

'Why?' The question had fallen from her lips unbidden.

His expression had flickered. 'Don't be tedious.'

He had sounded almost impatient, as though she were irritating him by presuming to question why he had asked her to have dinner with him when the answer was obvious.

That single glance when I stopped dancing. Cutting right into me. Deep inside...

That was all it had taken.

As she'd sat in the taxi, unconsciously pulling as far away from him as the confined space had permitted, it had been impossible to deny. Out of nowhere, a single glance from a stranger had— Had *what*, precisely?

She'd been burningly aware of his presence a bare few feet away, conscious of the faint but evocative scent of his aftershave, of the sheer masculinity of the man, of the length of his outstretched legs, of his hand casually resting on his powerful thigh. She'd looked doggedly ahead, aware of her tight grip on her clutch bag but somehow unable to relax it, aware of the pulse thudding in her throat, the tightness of her lungs, trying to keep her breathing natural as she'd gazed sightlessly ahead of her at the stop-start New York traffic and the city canyons crushing around them.

Heading off for dinner with a man who was a complete stranger.

Luca Farnese.

The name rang no bells, but clearly he was one of those people who moved in the same circles as the van Hurens—a banker or an investor or some such. She lifted her wine glass to her lips, still burningly aware of the man sitting opposite her. of the impact he was having on her, as she took in his chiselled profile, the blade of his nose, the high cheekbones, the sable hair, the line of his jaw. He was the whole damn package, from his lean, taut body to that subtly spiced aftershave and his intense, overpowering masculinity.

As to why—why him?—she still didn't know.

There were plenty of good-looking males in the world. But not a single one had ever had the effect on her that this one had—so that she'd upped and gone off with him when anything like that had been furthest from her intentions.

Well, why shouldn't I have dinner with him? I'm single and unattached. So what if I've only just met him?

Defiantly, her eyes flickered to him now, as she took a second jittery sip of wine. He was lifting his own glass.

'To an enjoyable evening,' he murmured, and his gaze, veiled and half-lidded, lingered on her fractionally before dipping as he took a leisurely appreciative mouthful of the doubtlessly expensive vintage wine.

She watched him savour it, then set down the glass, reaching for one of the poppy seed bread rolls in the silvered basket, tearing it open with his long, strong fingers, then spreading it with a curl of the yellow butter floating in an ice-water dish.

'So,' he began, glancing across at her, still with that half-lidded veil over his eyes, 'what took you to the van Hurens' this evening?'

The question was uttered in nothing more exceptional than a civilly polite voice, and Ariana was grateful. She needed to let the electric charge circling inside her dissipate. Conversation would do it.

'Mrs van Huren is a client of mine,' she answered.

They were speaking in English, and she was glad of that too. This was New York, and Italy was four thousand miles away.

And maybe I want to keep it four thousand miles away...

'Client?' Again, there was no more than civility in his question.

'I'm an interior designer. I recently did her house in the Hamptons.' Ariana answered with the same politeness that she might have used with any acquaintance. Or a complete stranger. 'She was kind enough to invite me to her birthday party tonight. I've just flown up from Florida, after doing some work for my mother there.'

'Interior design?' Luca Farnese said musingly, demolishing the last of the bread roll. 'Not my field. Tell me about it.'

There was a different note to his voice now. It was no less civil, but with a note of expectation in it that put it in the category of a business-based enquiry.

As if he were making an investment assessment, Ariana found herself thinking. Not that she required any investment funds. Nor would she ever seek them. She had not escaped her grandfather's hold only to put herself into the hands of control by investors.

Control by anyone, for any reason.

Her gaze flickered over him. Over the starkly good-looking face, where the hardness of his features was not softened in the slightest by being so ludicrously handsome, rather exacerbated…

If I ever did want investment funds—finance of any kind—you would be the very last man I would turn to.

There was an air of ruthlessness about him that she could sense. After all, hadn't he shown her that with his abrupt invitation to her tonight? Helping himself to something he wanted with little regard to the niceties of social discourse?

Every instinct told her that a man like that, surfacing from where she had no idea, would be a bad person to be beholden to. To be in his power…

She pulled her thoughts away. He'd asked a simple question—the kind that a man like him would ask about any business sector he was unfamiliar with—and she should answer him accordingly.

Their first course arrived—an assiette of *saumon fumé*—and she started to eat as she talked.

'What would you like to know?' she countered.

'Whatever you consider relevant,' he returned, attacking his smoked salmon. 'Do you work for yourself, or for a company?'

'The former,' she answered crisply. 'I would never work for anyone else!'

An assessing glance came her way. 'That sounds very definite. Can you afford that luxury?'

Ariana's mouth thinned. 'I make sure of it,' she said. 'I won't be dependent on anyone—or beholden to them.'

Even as she spoke she wondered at herself. Why on earth was she saying all that to a man she didn't know from Adam? Yet she was, all the same. And more.

'I'd rather starve in a gutter,' she said slowly. Unconsciously, she let her grip on her knife and fork tighten, and her jaw clenched.

Luca Farnese's dark, unreadable gaze rested on her, and he paused in his own eating. He said nothing for a moment, and then, 'You don't look like you're facing that possibility,' he observed, clearly taking in her expensive designer dress and overall chic appearance. His voice was very dry.

'I'm not,' she replied, her manner crisp again. 'I'm doing very comfortably, thank you.'

'Courtesy of the likes of Mrs van Huren…?'

'Yes, precisely.'

'Do you work only in North America?' Again, there was only cool enquiry in his voice.

'No, in Italy, mostly. I'm based in Tuscany. But I have clients here too. Some have properties in Italy as well—hence the link.'

'Where do you make the most money?'

'It's not a question of where, so much as from whom.' It was Ariana's turn to make her voice dry. 'Once I gain a client's trust and confidence, then she will often engage me for other properties, or to redo one I did some years ago.'

'So…' he glanced at her again as he resumed eating '…repeat business rather than growth of your client base?'

'Both.' Her voice was still crisp. 'There's a finite number of properties, even for very wealthy clients, no matter how often they're redone, so taking on new clients regularly is essential. I have to be careful, though, not to over-extend. Each client gets my exclusive attention, and I can't and won't dilute that.'

He frowned. 'You don't take on staff?'

'No—quite deliberately so. It would compromise my personal brand and give me headaches over management, employment law, et cetera. Even taking on freelance designers would be complicated, so I avoid it completely. I prefer it that way.'

'So what is your gross turnover?'

She blinked. 'And that would be your business because…?' she countered.

A thin smile indented his mouth briefly. 'Habit,' he said succinctly.

'Forgive me,' she said sweetly, 'if I don't satisfy your curiosity on that. Since I'm not a limited company, my accounts are my own business.'

A careless shrug of one shoulder was her answer. 'Like I said—habit.' A half-smile twisted at his mouth, not humorous so much as sardonic. 'I admit I find it curious to encounter someone who does not wish to expand their business or seek investment for such expansion.'

Ariana shrugged back. 'I'm comfortable where I am,' she said. 'I make a reasonable profit and, as you observed, I am not facing penury,' she added sweetly.

A waiter whisked away their empty plates and another deposited their entrées, while the sommelier reappeared to refresh their glasses. When they were finally left alone, Luca Farnese resumed his interrogation.

Why don't I mind him doing so?

The question fleeted through Ariana's thoughts, but she had an answer already. Several of them. Because it was giving them something to pass the time—a neutral subject that didn't matter.

But there was more to it than that, she realised. Memory stabbed of her pathetic attempts to get her grandfather to acknowledge her achievement in building a successful business from scratch. His response had been scathing. She would crash and burn, go bankrupt. It was inevitable—just a matter of time—she should have stuck to choosing colours and fabrics…

The old and all too familiar burning resentment rose in her, and with it came a realisation that she was actually enjoying being interrogated by someone like Luca Farnese. He was taking her seriously, doing her the courtesy of treating her like a businesswoman—not a silly little female, way out of her depth and making a fool of herself…

'How does your profit align with charging for your professional time? Or as against the uplift on what you supply to clients in material? And how do you manage cost differentials between suppliers and what you pass on to clients?' Luca Farnese was asking now, as both of them made a start on the succulent rich steaks of their *tournedos rossini*.

'Carefully!' Ariana acknowledged. 'I have to provide added value as a middleman, or my clients could go straight to the suppliers and vice versa. My USP is very often simply sourcing—knowing how to get what a client wants, from somewhere she hasn't thought of.'

'Do you carry inventory?'

'Some…but I have to be careful about that too,' Ariana answered.

'Dead money?'

'Yes, indeed. But it gives me agility and speed if I have something in stock that I know a particular client likes—I buy in anticipation sometimes.'

'Risky?' he observed laconically.

She nodded. 'That's why knowing my clients is key. I can sometimes be proactive—pre-emptive, even. If I see something—say, at an antiques sale—I can let a client know even if she hasn't considered that she wants it. Knowing my clients' tastes intimately is a big part of my value, and it helps keep them loyal to me.'

He went on to his next question, and Ariana realised she was finding it a stimulating experience. His line of questioning was keen, and without doubt reflected a surgical precision when it came to grasping the anatomy of any business. Interior design would be small fry to someone like him, of course.

Deciding she'd had enough of being the one under interrogation, she turned the tables. 'So, what about you? What do you do to keep yourself from penury?'

She made her voice light, but pointed for all that, to make it clear that she was done with this one-way discourse.

He looked at her speculatively. As if assessing her.

Does he think I should know who he is?

She took him on. 'The world of high finance, which I assume is your field, since you are a business acquaintance of Charles van Huren, is as unknown to me as interior design is to you,' she said to him.

'I invest,' he said shortly. 'I also speculate.'

Ariana raised her eyebrows. 'Risky?' she observed, deliberately using the word he'd applied to her earlier.

A curt shake of his head came her way. 'Hedged,' he said.

'Ah…' she took another mouthful of the melt-in-the-mouth tender fillet '…one of those!'

His mouth thinned. She could see it.

She knew he was about to speak, but she pre-empted him. 'I know…' Her voice was very dry, the look in her eye drier still. *"Don't be tedious?"* She eyed him. 'You were going to say that again, weren't you?'

'In my experience…' and Luca Farnese's voice was even drier than hers '…those who deride hedge funds are those who can't afford to invest in them or make the profits they bring.'

'Well,' she acknowledged consideringly, 'I have no complaints to make. I earn my money from women who are rich enough to afford beautiful homes, and you and your kind are very often those who make the money to pay for those beautiful homes.'

She gave a half-smile as she spoke, meeting his gaze. Feeling its power. Wondering at it. And wondering, with almost a sense of confusion, just what it was about him that made her so physically…sexually… aware of him.

She'd known better-looking men, flirtatious and openly admiring, with handsome faces and good bodies—had even dated some of them when she hadn't been busy on client projects. But not a single one of them had possessed the dark, powerful allure that this man did.

She was ultra-aware of him—everything about him. From the way his cropped hair feathered slightly at the nape of his neck to the faint sign of incipient regrowth at this hour of the evening along the strong line of his jaw, the way he wore his charcoal business suit and the thin wrap of gold around his wrist in the understated but formidably expensive watch, the equally understated studs of his cufflinks.

But it wasn't the external things about him, nor even the darkly saturnine looks—it was more. Dangerously more…

It was the knowledge that the only reason she was here, having this unplanned, unscheduled dinner with him, was that he was responding to her in exactly the same way as she was to him. She wouldn't be here otherwise…

It was both a heady sensation and a disturbing one.

This has come out of nowhere. Two hours ago I'd never set eyes on him. Yet here I am, dining with him.

Dining—and what else…?

She slid the question aside. Unwilling, right now, to face it, let alone answer it. Instead, she asked a different one aloud—one to keep the conversation going.

'So…' she sliced off another delicious sliver of tender beef, dunking it in the rich, truffle-based sauce '…what about you? Do you have a base? Or are you one of those globe-trotting financier types?' She made her voice sound politely interested.

'I operate out of Milan,' he supplied.

'Milan I could live in, at a pinch,' she said musingly. 'But New York never. Far too modern, too frenetic.'

'I agree. But don't you care for Milan?'

She shook her head. 'Not really,' she conceded. 'Tuscany suits me better. I've lived in Central Italy all my life—my mother's family is from there.'

She knew there was an automatic constraint in her voice. She did not want to think about either her mother or her grandfather, in his opulent *palazzo* in Tuscany's neighbour Umbria. It was a luxurious prison for those her grandfather wanted to keep at heel. But her mother had escaped—rackety though her lifestyle was—and she too had escaped.

Only her cousin was still trapped. Poor little Mia, her

grandfather's captive. Pampered and petted and kept in a cage she dared not break out of.

I offered her a way out—said she could come and live with me, work with me—but she turned it down. Didn't dare. Didn't want to lose our grandfather's approval.

She could not blame her. Mia had seen first-hand their grandfather's rage and his contempt for the granddaughter who had dared to break away from his control. Mia wasn't strong, as she was. Her meekness, her timidity, her gentleness—all counted against her when it came to breaking free.

She shook her head clear of thoughts that were useless. She could not help—not until there was something Mia actually wanted from her.

Luca Farnese was speaking again, and her attention went back to him.

'Killane...' he murmured. 'No other links to Ireland?'

'No,' Ariana said shortly.

She knew nothing about her father, other than the fact that he'd been good-looking, feckless, and had readily accepted a pay-off from her grandfather to accede to a speedy divorce the moment she'd been born. Where he was now was of no interest to her. Just as she had never been of any interest to him. Nor to her mother either.

She gave a mental shrug. She was used to not being wanted—neither by her parents nor her grandfather.

But one day I will be wanted—one day there will be a special person for me.

Who it would be she had no idea, but he was out there somewhere...

Her gaze came back to Luca Farnese. Something was

happening between them…something that was impossible to deny, but that had been there from that first electrifying moment. She felt a frisson go through her. What had seared through her when he'd watched her dance—what she was burningly aware of in her every moment in his company—was like nothing she had ever encountered before…experienced before.

Could this be...? Could this possibly be...?

The question was trying to form in her head, but she would not let it. Too soon, too difficult…and far too uncertain…

Yet she felt strange currents swirling inchoate within her, bringing to the surface thoughts, wonderings, questions…

Her eyes went to him again as she cleared her plate and pushed it away, replete after the rich, delicious food, reaching for her wine glass. Against her own expectations she had relaxed—partly under the stimulation of describing her line of business, partly because this was her second glass of wine, and partly due to a new awareness taking shape in her, because he wanted her to relax.

Her expression flickered now. *It's why he got me on to interior design. Knowing I'd let my guard down on a subject familiar to me, something I'm so involved with...*

A question hovered in her head. *And just why does he want me to relax...?*

She didn't need to answer that. It was in the way his eyes were meeting hers, the way he was reaching for his own wine glass, taking an answering mouthful. Holding her eyes just a little bit longer than the conversation between them warranted.

Beneath the surface something quite different is happening...

His unreadable dark gaze rested on her and she felt a sudden hollow open up inside her. It was not unreadable at all. She felt her stomach clench, her throat tighten. Her pulse quickened and her eyes widened. It was impossible to prevent the tell-tale revealing dilation of her pupils.

As if a switch had been thrown, the rest of the restaurant disappeared and all the people in it. They simply vanished. Only this man was here—Luca Farnese, sitting opposite her, his long body lounging back, setting down his wine glass with a click on the table, leaning forward, reaching a hand out…

In a slow, leisurely manner, he traced across her cheek with one fingertip, from her cheekbone to the corner of her mouth.

'Stay with me tonight,' he said.

His voice was low. Husky.

His dark eyes were neither hard nor soft.

Only desiring…

CHAPTER THREE

LUCA FELT HIS gaze narrowing, pupils flaring. An instinctive, unstoppable reaction. As instinctive as the lift of his hand as he'd reached forward and made contact with that soft-sheened skin across which he had drawn the tip of his finger, to touch lightly…so lightly…on the swell of her lower lip. Then drop away.

He reached for his wine glass. Took a slow, leisurely draft, never dropping his eyes from her. He watched her face, watched the expression in her deep smoky eyes change. Saw her full, lush lips part slightly, heard an almost inaudible inhalation of her breath. Giving him the only answer he needed.

He felt his body quicken. Yielding to what he'd been keeping supressed—leashed—as he'd reverted with calculated determination to business, the subject he found easiest to talk about, even applied to a sector he was unfamiliar with.

It had served its purpose. Got them to this point.

To the decision he'd just made.

He wanted her.

It didn't matter that he didn't want to want her…that nothing about this tonight should be happening.

It was too late for such thoughts. What was happening was happening, and it was overriding everything else. Overriding all caution, all reluctance, all wariness. All reason.

Ruthlessly he put them all aside. Just as he had from the first moment he'd set eyes on her, sensuously dancing in a world of her own, drawing his eyes to her, dominating his focus. His response to her overrode them all.

His eyes rested on her now, feeling the power of her allure. Her mane of dark burnished hair, the deep smoky eyes, the lush mouth. Her ripe, rich beauty. A slow, potent curl of desire went through him. His body quickened again, arousal cresting in him, more powerful, more visceral than he had ever known.

His eyes washed over her. The dress that moulded her body was in the way—he wanted it gone. Wanted to see her full breasts spill free of it, wanted to peel it from her like a ripe fruit, to feast on what was concealed within.

He moved, restless suddenly, summoning the waiter, scrawling his name on the tab. He was known here. The invoice would be sent to his office for settlement. Then he was getting to his feet. Forgoing the usually required social civilities of asking whether she might like dessert, coffee, liqueurs. He had no time for that now.

Desire was unleashed in him—insistent and imperative. It shouldn't be there, but it was, and he didn't care that this was not what he should be doing, that this woman had no place in his life. That he should never have looked at her, should never have taken her to dinner. Should not now be intent on taking her back to his hotel.

I should put her in a taxi, send her off—consign her to nothing more than passing memory.

But he didn't want to.

Not now.

Not yet.

There was only one thing he wanted, and his hunger for it was increasing every moment.

'Let's go.'

He drew her to her feet, draping her jacket around her shoulders.

Out on the pavement, he turned to her. 'My hotel is on this block,' he said.

She made no reply, and he did not require one. All he required now was for her to do what she was doing. Walking beside him along the near-deserted sidewalk, not speaking against the traffic noise, her hands holding her jacket together, holding her clutch bag, keeping pace with his long stride on her high heels.

The charge between them now was so strong that it was like St Elmo's Fire, flaring around them.

Inside the lobby of the boutique hotel—small, discreet, ultra-luxurious and exactly the way he liked it—he guided her to the elevator. Still she said nothing, and neither did he. There was no purpose now in further speech.

Yet in the confines of the elevator he could hear her breathing, sense the tension in her. A tension he shared. Arousal was scything through him, blotting out everything else. He wanted to reach for her, release the tension racking within him. He was holding himself apart from her by sheer strength of will. Refusing to let himself even look at her as he stood beside her as the elevator soared upwards. Taking them to the only place he wanted her to be.

His bed.

Faintness drummed through Ariana. Not from the wine she'd drunk at dinner, nor the champagne at Maisie van Huren's party, nor even the upward whoosh of the elevator.

From what she was doing. And why.

Because there was only one 'why' in what she was doing. Though it made no sense. She did not do things like this. She did not go back to the hotel room of a man she had only just met. But she was doing it now.

With Luca Farnese.

But why? Why him? Why this man?

The question thrummed in her head, as it had all evening. Her eyes went to him. Fastened on him. On the aquiline profile, the sculpted cheekbones and the hard-edged jawline that was already darkening, the long-lashed deep-set eyes and the sensual mouth, the lines etched around it.

Drawing her as no man ever had before…

Knowledge flooded into her. Knowledge of exactly what she was doing—and why.

Because I want to. Because out of nowhere he's walked into my life, and for reasons I can't understand he has a power, a sexual potency I've never experienced!

But did she want to experience it? Did she want that

dark allure of his to draw her closer? Did she want to give herself to its embrace?

She felt a sensation like electricity flicker along her nerves, felt the pulse at her throat start to race. Something she did not know—had never known—had happened as she'd lifted her head after the hypnotic rhythm on the dance floor, her gaze clashing with his. She had acknowledged that something was flowing between them. Impossible to deny. Primitive and primeval.

It was here again, now, in this confined space. Pressing all around her. Her and him. They did not speak, and he was not looking at her, but she could sense, palpably, the restraint he was exerting. It was visible in the set of his jaw, the compression of his mouth, the tension across his shoulders.

He's leashed—leashing the power he wants to exert. That he wants to release.

She felt the voltage of the electricity that was building up around them, between them, as if she were in the middle of a charged space, heat beating up inside her, flushing through her veins.

It was madness—she knew that. Knew that even now she should stop what was happening. She should break the electric silence, turn to him and say, *Actually, I'd better go back to my own hotel, I think.* Halt the elevator and send it back to the lobby. Get into a taxi and leave without a backward glance. Alone.

Leaving Luca Farnese to be nothing more than a fleeting memory of a single night in New York, having dinner with him and then walking away. Going back to Italy…back to her normal, predictable life. Familiar. Safe.

Yes, she would do it. She would do just that. The moment the elevator stopped she would do it. She would turn to the man beside her, whose dark presence was as tangible as if his hand were fastened around her wrist, whose aftershave was still catching at her senses, whose obsidian eyes she could feel slicing through her. She would turn and say that she was sorry, that she had made a mistake…

She felt her heart thudding, her breathing quicken, every muscle taut. The elevator stopped with the slightest judder. The doors slid open. She began to turn, to tell Luca Farnese what she must tell him…

A hand slid around her hand. Cool, strong fingers closing over hers. Silencing the words that died on her lips.

His head was turning to finally look down at her. His eyes held hers. Those dark, unbearable, obsidian eyes… cutting into the very heart of her. Telling her nothing. Telling her everything.

Her breath stopped—her heart stopped.

Desire, like black fire, shone in the depths of his blacker eyes… Burning towards her like a black flame—a flame that consumed all that was reason and sense. Burning away everything but what was now left to her—a knowledge that was deeper than reason or sense.

This is what I want.

This was what had been engendered from the very moment she had seen him looking at her and felt him reach into the very core of her.

'Come,' he said, and his voice was low, insistent.

His cool, strong fingers meshed with hers, leading her forward to the only place she wanted to be now… tonight… She knew that with a certainty that burned away everything else in the world, in existence.

In Luca Farnese's arms.

His bed.

Luca watched her enter the room as he stepped in behind her, shutting the door and flicking on the two bedside lamps to bathe the room in a soft, low light. She was standing there, in the middle of the room. Not moving. Her eyes were huge, and smoky, and fixed on him.

He felt desire—arousal—kick inside him, hot and urgent. He was behaving as he had never done. Picking up a woman at a party just to have sex with her.

He thrust the crude description aside. Who the hell cared how they had got here, or how swiftly? It would be one night—one night only. One night of breaking every rule in his book.

Especially now...when you are on the brink of making a quite different life for yourself.

He thrust aside the warning that was trying to gain entrance. He didn't have time for it, nor room for it. Instead, he let his eyes feast on the woman standing there, full breasts straining beneath the fabric of her dress, hair a fall of satin and silk around her shoulders like a veil, parting to display the sensual beauty of her face.

Displaying it for him.

Displaying herself.

He walked towards her…halted. Her eyes were huge,

lifted to his, fire flaring in their smoky depths. Her lips had parted and he could hear her breathe. See the pulse throbbing at her slender throat…

He slid his hand around it, thumb resting on her pulse, feeling it throb beneath her skin, feeling her tremble at his touch. He let his hand relax, easing it down sensuously to graze his thumb along the delicate length of her collarbone. He reached his other hand forward, trailed his index finger slowly, deliberately, down her cheek, seeing her pupils dilate, feeling the fine, subliminal tremble of her body again.

His hand slid over her shoulder, moulding the flesh beneath as he turned her around. He smoothed the fall of her tumbling hair from her back and she dipped her head forward. She knew what he was doing…what he was about to do. He could feel her still trembling, quivering, motionless though she appeared.

With a single unbroken movement he drew down the zip of her dress. As he did so, slipping the fastening of her bra, arousal flared in him more strongly, more urgently yet. He slid his hands inside the dress, around her body, beneath her bra. Cupping her breasts as they spilled into his palms.

She gave a gasp, head thrown back, and he began to pluck at the nipples, engorging at his touch. Blood surged in his body and she gasped again, head rolling. He gave a low laugh, his body responding as fully to hers as hers did to his, and pulled her back against him. The curves of her hips fitted against him, desire cresting at the lush softness of her against the hardening of his own body.

For a moment…a totally self-indulgent moment…he kept her there…

Then he released her, stepping away.

'I'll use the bathroom,' he told her, turning away, striding in, shutting the door behind him.

He took his time, methodically stripping off his clothes, draping them over the shower rail, putting his shoes beneath the vanity. The process gave him the pause he needed. The control he needed. Yet he could feel a nerve working in his cheek, knew how tightly his jaw was tensed, how focussed his gaze was as he reached for a towel to snake it around his hips.

For one long second he saw his own reflection.

It was that of a stranger.

I don't do this. I don't pick up women at parties and bring them back to my hotel room. I don't do it.

And to do it now—at this juncture of his life…

So why? Why was he doing it?

The question burned, demanding and accusing.

He got his answer as he walked out of the bathroom.

She was lying in the bed, half exposed by the pulled-back bedding, and her lush, ripe body was waiting for him.

For his possession.

The sheet was cold beneath Ariana's naked back and she welcomed it. Her body was a blaze of heat. Filled with an insanity she could not subdue. Because surely she was insane, to be doing this? Coming to the hotel room of a man she had never set eyes on before this evening?

She felt defiance spear through her. She was giving herself to this moment and she would not question why. A stranger he might be, but what was burning between them she could not—would not—be denied. Or resisted…

He is like no one I have ever known before! Whatever it is about him, it draws me to him. I just want him so, so much... I want him to want me and desire me... because I am burning with desire for him...

Restlessly, she moved her naked body on the cold sheet, arousal blazing in her. She had never, ever, felt it so strongly before.

Only now—with this man—he's setting me alight...

Anticipation, hunger, the longing for him, for his touch, his possession, made her breathing shallow, her heart race. She felt her arousal mount. Where was he? What was keeping him? She wanted him—she wanted him *now…*

And then, with a leap in her heart, a catch in her throat, she saw he was there. Walking out of the bathroom, his torso hard and muscled, wearing nothing but a towel snaked around his hips, which could not disguise the fact that what was possessing him was just as powerful.

His eyes were fixed on her, dark, and purposeful. He stopped by the bed, looked down at her. Her breasts were bare—there seemed little point in modesty now…not after his shocking, intimate possession of them. Her nipples were crested coral peaks, straining upwards above the sheet pulled across her.

Until he lifted it away.

He looked down at her completely naked body. His

gaze seared her. Then in a single movement he had flung aside his towel and slid his smooth, powerful body, naked and aroused, down beside her, to start his possession of her. His complete and total possession…

Light was pressing on Ariana's eyelids. Bright and insistent. She didn't want it, but could not turn it off. Something had woken her—some noise. She opened her eyes, blinking, saw sunlight diffused through the window of the room.

The hotel room she'd just spent the night in.

With Luca Farnese.

She stilled, heat flushing through her naked body. Consciousness burning in her of the night she had just spent with him.

Dear God, did I really do it? Did I really fall into bed with him the very evening I met him? Fall into bed with him and have sex so abandoned, so intense, so absolutely incredible that I can't believe it was possible...

But how could she deny it? Or want to deny it…

It had been amazing, fantastic! Taking her to a plane of sensuality she hadn't known existed, had never known could exist! Just as, she felt her breath catch with wonder, Luca Farnese was a man she had never known could exist…not outside her dreams and longings.

She turned, reaching instinctively for him. Wanting to be in his arms again, to hold him close—hold this most incredible man, who had suddenly appeared in her life, setting her on fire for him….

A man, she realised, with a sudden hollowing of her stomach, who was no longer beside her in the bed.

She jolted herself up on her elbows, staring around. There was no one there. The room was empty. The only clothing visible was her own—her discarded dress and underwear on the chair where she'd left them.

Emptiness filled the room. The en suite bathroom door stood open…the room was empty. She jack-knifed up, feeling her muscles and limbs protest at the sudden movement.

Limbs that had strained with their every fibre against the hardness of his.

Her hands had clung to his back, his shoulders, his hips, indenting deeply. Her neck and throat had arched as her spine had arched, as orgasm after orgasm had exploded through her, and her voice had cried out with it.

Memory drenched through her like scalding water and she gave a cry, her hand flying to her mouth. Between her legs a dull ache was throbbing, low and persistent. Testimony she could not deny.

Just as the empty room was testimony.

She stared around, feeling her heart start to thud with apprehension. Disbelief. Dismay.

Slowly, very slowly, she stood up, heart thudding more heavily. She looked about her. Apart from her clothes, the only thing she saw was her clutch bag on the unit beside the TV. And the note propped against the screen.

With shaking hands she snatched it up, opened it. Read the brief, curt words incised on the paper.

I have to go. Room service is on the tab for breakfast. I wish you well.

He'd signed it with his initials. *LF.* That was all.

She let the note fall from her hand. Numbly, still disbelieving that he had gone, she walked into the en suite bathroom, unhooked the towelling robe there and thrust her arms into it, knotting it tightly around her body. She could feel the thudding of her heart become a hammering. Feel nausea rising in her.

Like an automaton she crossed the bedroom, bare feet sinking into the carpet, pulling open the door with nerveless fingers as she registered, belatedly, what the noise that had woken her had been.

Luca Farnese leaving. Walking out on her.

As if what had happened was nothing—*nothing...*

She stepped into the corridor, saw him standing a few metres away by the elevator.

'Why?'

The single word fell from her lips.

He turned, his expression masked.

He did not bother to ask her what she meant.

'Last night was a mistake.'

His voice was curt and clipped.

'A mistake?' Ariana's voice was hollow.

An impatient look crossed his face.

'It should not have happened,' he said. His mouth thinned. 'If you had any…expectations…please accept my regrets for the misunderstanding.'

Ariana's face convulsed. But he was not done yet.

'I wish you well,' he said. 'However, I can have nothing more to do with you.'

Her eyes were distended, her voice a bare husk.

'Why…?'

The single word came again, as if it had been ground from her out of broken glass.

The impatient look was on his face again—and something more. Absolute rejection.

'I'm returning to Italy today.'

He took a razoring breath. Eyes levelled on her, cutting into hers.

'I'm getting married,' he said.

Luca sat immobile in the hotel limousine driving him to JFK International Airport. His fingers gripped into the leather of the seat's armrest. In his head a scene was replaying. That tableau in the elevator lobby outside his hotel suite.

For a second—a fraction of a second—she'd held herself completely motionless, wrapped in a bathrobe, hair tumbling over her shoulders, face stark, after he'd said what he'd had to say...given her his reason for walking out on her as he had. Then a cry had been wrenched from her—a hoarse, gasping sound—and every feature had contorted. She'd started forward, hands clenched, hurling words at him like bullets sprayed from a machine gun.

'You *bastard*! You total, absolute bastard! You piece of—'

That broken cry had come again, and then she'd been surging forward, hands raised, closing the short distance between them to where he stood, rigid and rejecting, by the elevator doors. She'd pummelled his chest and he had seized her wrists, holding her away with main force and a face as black as night. She had tried to wrench her hands free, twisting her body frantically, repeating her denunciation of him, yelling at him, her eyes ablaze with fury.

And fury had seized him too. Fury that had come from somewhere very deep inside. From a place he'd never before allowed to get control of him. But which had possessed him then.

He had not spoken, only thrust her away, releasing her wrists as the elevator doors had opened. The car had been occupied, with hotel guests coming down from a higher floor, and he'd seen them react to the woman hurling vitriol at him, with her tangled hair all over the place, wild-eyed, features contorted, barefoot and wearing a bathrobe all but coming apart at her cleavage. He'd seen their shock, their embarrassment.

She'd still been yelling at him, but his own black, ice-cold fury had deafened him to it. He'd stepped back, moving into the elevator car as the doors sliced shut, blocking her out. Silencing her.

His rage had been absolute.

It still was.

With her, and with someone who was even more culpable than the yelling banshee he'd thrust away from him.

With himself.

For the criminal stupidity of what he'd done.

Ariana sank down on the bed, its crumpled sheets cruelly, viciously mocking her. She was shaking…shaking all over…her legs like straw, her body weak, as if she were made of tissue paper.

She felt eviscerated—as if talons had ripped her open. Humiliation seared through her like a wash of burning acid. To have done what she had—let herself be used as Luca Farnese had used her, so shamelessly, so ruthlessly, for a night of sordid sexual gratification! An empty, meaningless encounter that he'd *known* was to be nothing more—*could* be nothing more!

He had known all along. From the very first moment when he'd stood looking at her as she danced…to the moment he'd walked out on her, leaving her, used and discarded, in his tumbled bed.

In her head, his cold, dismissive words stabbed like an icy knife.

'I'm getting married.'

Those words had consigned her, in that instant, to being little better than a prostitute. And condemned himself, beyond any excuse, to being what she had told him he was, hurled at him in her rage and humiliation…

She wrapped her arms around her body as if to hold herself together.

He deserved it! He deserved every word I threw at him!

And she—oh, she deserved the other word burning in her throat. Choking her.

Fool. Fool, fool, fool…

To have done what she had done…

Yet even as she knew that, she knew something else too—something that cried from her. Something she dared not admit to…

That she wanted, with all her being, for him to have

been the man she'd thought he was when she'd been in his arms.

Not who he'd proved—so cruelly and so callously—to be…

CHAPTER FOUR

LUCA SAT AT his desk in his Milan office, his expression stark. He *must* put behind him the insanity of the act he'd committed in New York. That night of sex with a woman so unlike any other he had ever been with. Sex so intense, so…so *torrid*—the hackneyed term twisted his mouth—and so explosive that it could still, a week later, burn in his head like a flaming brand.

Only sanity had prevailed. He had walked out on her. And when he had—when he'd stood by that elevator—he'd endured what he never intended to endure again. Her face twisted with explosive rage as she hurled her accusations. Her vitriolic condemnation of him. And behind him the shocked embarrassment of the occupants of the hotel elevator as they witnessed the scene.

Memory came from much longer ago. His mother, not caring who saw her in her rages. His father enduring it all, long-suffering, brow-beaten, doing nothing to stop the hideous scenes, endlessly trying to placate her, plead with her, making no difference at all to the way she behaved… And himself as a young boy, cowering, hating it, wanting his mother to stop—stop raging, stop being so *angry.* Wanting her only to hold out her arms to him… But she never, ever did. Never had…

He felt emotion from long, long ago clench within him.

Emotion from much more recently.

Both toxic.

His jaw steeled, eyes hardening. He would consign Ariana Killane and the disastrous night he'd spent with her to oblivion. Only one woman mattered—the woman of his dreams. The woman he was going to marry. And this very weekend he would stake his claim to her.

There was only one woman, from now on, whom he would ever permit to exist for him.

And it was not—*not*—Ariana Killane.

Ariana stepped back, staring at her colour board. With a frown of concentration she removed one of the fabric swatches pinned to it, replacing it with another from the clutch she held in her left hand. Yes, that was better. She reached for her camera, reeling off shots to send to her client, together with her detailed proposal.

It would take her till late this evening to complete it, together with the costings and timeframes, but she welcomed the work. Since returning from New York she'd done everything in her power not to let herself remember what had happened there. Yet every time she lost focus on work memory leapt—every searing detail of that unforgettable night…

Until she crashed and burned on the memory of what had come after it.

That was all she should allow herself to remember!

That hideous morning-after, when Luca Farnese had shown her just what the night had meant to him.

Nothing—less than nothing…

A mistake. That had been his curt dismissal of it.

Whereas for her…

She felt an ache possess her—an ache for something she tried so hard not to admit. An ache for what had never happened…

And yet it haunted her still with longing.

Waking in his arms, seeing him smiling at me, him kissing me, warmth in his eyes... Ordering breakfast—breakfast in bed—making love again afterwards... Then getting up and dressed...wandering hand in hand through Central Park...finding somewhere to have lunch. We'd talk about ourselves and tell each other everything, laugh and kiss... And he would tell me how glad he was we'd found each other, how amazing our night together was, how special I was to him...

Instead—

'I'm getting married.'

That was what he had said to her. It had been the indifference of his dismissal, the coldness in his face, his voice—the callousness of what he'd done to her—that had made her call him out for what he was, and her words had been as accurate as they were crude, as she'd hurled them at him in her fury.

The recollection of her blind, humiliated rage was her only comfort now—all that she could cling to along with the shreds of her self-respect. Yet it could not assuage the accusation still lacerating her, the knowledge of her own stupidity and the folly of what she had done.

Her expression hardened, face tightening. Well, she had learnt a lesson, that was for sure! One of the many in her life she'd learnt about not being wanted, not being valued.

Like her father wanting only her grandfather's money, not the daughter he had conceived. Like her mother preferring whoever her latest husband was to her daughter, jaunting off and leaving her with the grandfather who had only ever found fault with her. Like the grandfather so scathing in his condemnation of everything about her, with his endless unfavourable comparisons with her cousin, so meek and docile.

Like being used as some kind of disposable throwaway sex toy by Luca Farnese, before he headed back to the woman he was going to marry.

Her mouth twisted. Did that unknown woman know what kind of man she was going to marry? She pitied her, whoever she was. No woman deserved Luca Farnese. Not for a husband. Or for anything else…

Not even for a one-night stand in New York. For that, least of all.

'Signor Farnese—it is good to see you again. How is our business venture progressing?'

The elderly man rising with some difficulty from his armchair in the book-lined library of the resplendent Renaissance *palazzo* in Umbria was warm in his greeting.

Luca's handshake was brief and firm, and he waited politely for the elderly man to resume his seat before taking his own. For the next few minutes he made the required report to his host. His demeanour was respectful, given that Tomaso Castellani, even in his eighties, was a financial force to be reckoned with. But he knew that his own investment in the long-established Castellani import/export empire, broadening it into China and the Far East, was of greater value to his host than to himself.

But then, his interest in Castellani SpA was not confined to business matters.

It hadn't been from the very first time he'd come to the *palazzo*, some six weeks ago, at Tomaso's invitation, to explore the possibility of a business association between them. Lunch had followed their preliminary discussion—and it had put the matter all but out of his head.

There had been one simple, life-changing reason for that.

The angelically fair young woman who had walked into the ornate dining room as they took their places, her quiet manner as diffident as her smile was shy and sweet, her hesitant, low-pitched voice as melodious as her eyes were celestial blue, dipping downwards demurely as Tomaso performed his introductions.

From the moment he'd set eyes on her he had been lost, Luca knew. Captivated. This…*this* was the woman who had been in his dreams since his teenage years.

And now, today, he was going to make that dream a reality.

He felt his muscles tighten suddenly, as if a shot of adrenaline had surged through him.

And he would leave behind him, completely and permanently, all trace of that disastrous mistake he'd made in New York—and the woman he'd made it with. Who was out of his life—removed from it as precipitously as she'd entered it.

It was in the past, that night, and it was going to stay there. Locked away. Never, *never* to crawl back out.

It was one night—one night only out of all the years of my life! One night and one mistake. And it is over, finished—done with. All it has achieved is to make me surer than ever about what I want...the kind of woman I want. The absolute opposite of that one.

He wanted the woman who right now, at this very moment, was within his reach. And as he spoke to Tomaso Castellani, knowing what he said would come as no surprise to him, the approving, welcoming response of the elderly man only confirmed it—for why would he *not* be welcomed as so eligible a *parti*?

Genially, his face wreathed in smiles, Luca's host got to his feet, reaching for the silver-handled walking stick beside his chair. 'Come, my friend. First we shall lunch and then…' his smile deepened '…you have both my permission and my blessing, to make your proposal! And I do not doubt for a moment what her answer will be, so dear to me as she is.'

Nor did Luca doubt the answer he would receive. She was the woman of his dreams and he would devote his life to her and to her happiness. For him, no other woman would exist. None *could* exist.

For a fraction of a second memory flickered… Another woman—searing his senses…

He crushed it to oblivion. That woman no longer existed. He would not allow her to.

* * *

Ariana's expression was troubled as she stared frowningly at her phone. Mia did not often get in touch with her. It was not that they had grown apart, but it was difficult for Mia to see much of her, if anything at all. Ariana was not welcome at their grandfather's *palazzo*, and the more successful she was in her business the more unwelcome she was. It was a thorn in his flesh that she was not financially dependent on him.

Had it made him even more possessive of Mia? she wondered bleakly. Even more controlling of her cousin? Had her own escape from their grandfather's domination only increased that which he held over Mia? Although Mia had always been willing to be as meek and dutiful as their grandfather insisted, was she still content to be so?

If you can bear it, please, please come and visit, Ariana! So much has happened, and I long to see you again. I feel very alone just now.

Ariana's troubled expression deepened, and she searched her diary for a possible date for a visit. It would be tricky, for her diary was solid with work. Deliberately so. It helped to keep at bay the tormenting, humiliating memories that assailed her.

No! Don't got there! Just don't! You think that night with Luca Farnese was special because it wasn't something you'd ever done before. To light up like that, to fall into bed with a man you'd only just met just because he looked at you the way he did...touched you the way he did...made love to you the way he did...

Her mouth twisted. She was fantasising again! Luca Farnese hadn't 'made love' to her! He'd had sex with her—hot, torrid, searing, mind-blowing sex! She'd been a body to him—nothing more than that. A woman to sate his passing lust upon. A convenient female happy to roll into the sack with him—a last fling for a man before he hitched himself for life to another woman.

Her expression darkened even more. For him to indulge himself in a sex-fuelled one-night stand knowing…*knowing*…that he was going to be married, having committed himself to another woman and still thinking it was OK to tumble a stranger into bed… That… Oh, that was beyond despicable…

She dragged her angry thoughts away, focussing back on Mia. Her cousin needed her. Sudden decision filled her. If she dropped everything now, she could be at the *palazzo* in an hour or so.

Resolved, she texted back to her cousin. A moment later Mia's reply came. She sounded eager. More than eager.

Desperate.

Ariana's frown deepened.

Luca eased the gears of his car, a top-of-the-range sleek, silver-grey saloon, and moved off along the long gravel drive away from Tomaso's *palazzo*. Satisfaction filled him. And much more than that.

Relief—was that what he was feeling? Relief that he had finally achieved what he had longed for all his life?

Ahead, the wrought-iron gates, electronically controlled, started to open. But it wasn't because he was leaving. A car was turning into the drive, an open-topped sports car of a type popular with female drivers, in an eye-catching royal blue. It threw up gravel as it made the turn, accelerating forward to pass his car by. The driver was, as he'd expected, a woman, wearing a bright red suit, her head covered by a matching scarf. She had on huge sunglasses, her hands on the wheel in red leather gloves. She drove fast and purposefully, ignoring his presence.

He slowed to let her by, then found his eyes going to his rear-view mirror as she disappeared towards the *palazzo*. He frowned. Had there been something familiar about her?

He dismissed the thought, turning on to the highway and thinking no more about it. Dwelling, instead, on the woman from whom he'd just taken his leave.

His brand-new, absolutely perfect fiancée.

His ideal woman.

'What have *you* come here for?'

Ariana's grandfather's voice was harsh, his demand far from welcoming her arrival. Ariana shrugged, ignoring his reproof—because what else could she do?—peeling off her red driving gloves and removing her dark glasses.

'Mia asked me,' she replied, keeping her tone equable.

She tried not to rile her grandfather, though she knew that her very presence—her very existence—did so. She was after all, she thought, with a mingled stab of bitterness and pain, living proof of his errant daughter's unforgivable folly in not doing what he'd wanted her to do—making a suitable and well-bred match of his choosing. She had run away with a feckless wastrel instead.

Her grandfather's expression changed. Became pleased instead of disapproving. 'Hah! So she has told you her news? Well, go and congratulate her!'

Ariana halted in mid-removal of her headscarf. 'Congratulate her?' she echoed in a hollow voice.

'Of course! She is to be married!'

Her grandfather's voice was rich with approval. With satisfaction.

'Married?' Ariana felt shock reverberate through her. 'I had no idea…' she said limply.

Was this why she texted me? It must be—but she gave no hint of it!

Mixed emotions jarred within her. If Mia was getting married, that would explain why she longed to see her, as she'd put in her email. Ariana frowned. But then why would she have added *I feel very alone just now*?

'Where is she?' she asked her grandfather.

'Out in the garden—the gazebo,' her grandfather replied. Adding, 'The ideal place for a girl to receive a proposal!' he added, still in that voice registering strong approval.

Ariana's eyes widened. 'She's just got engaged *now*?' she asked.

'Yes, yes!' Her grandfather nodded irritably. His expression tightened. 'And it is as well you did not come any earlier. I would not have had her fiancé set eyes on *you*! He left just in time.'

Refusing to feel stung by her grandfather's criticism of her—when had she ever pleased him?—Ariana made the connection his words had instigated. That car she'd passed on her way in—sleek, black, with tinted windows. Her cousin's fiancé…

So, who?

Well, she wouldn't ask her grandfather.

Telling him she'd go and find Mia, she headed through the series of wide French windows opening off the grand *saloni* to the *terrazzo* beyond. The gazebo was situated on the edge of the huge stone pond, overlooking the regimented gardens with their straight pathways, severely clipped topiary and classical statues—not a garden for running about in or playing. But then her grandfather had considered any outdoor activity to be unfeminine, other than sedate walks up and down the gravelled paths.

The gazebo, at least, had been regarded as an acceptable destination, provided she and Mia had taken a suitable book with them to read there. Sometimes, when he had been particularly pleased with Mia, she'd been allowed to take her dolls and have a pretend tea party. Only when Mia had begged—prettily and gratefully—had Ariana been allowed to share in such a treat.

Ariana's expression was poignant. Mia had always been a sweet, sensitive soul. And she still was, Ariana knew only too well.

Please, please, let this engagement be welcome to her! Please let her text have been so agitated simply because she's feeling emotionally overwhelmed!

'Ariana, you came!' Mia's greeting was a cry, and she

leapt up from where she'd been sitting, gazing out over the parterre, and ran towards her.

Her hug was tight—and clinging. But when she released her Ariana saw, with a shock of dismay, that she'd been crying.

And they were not tears of joy, as a newly engaged woman's should be, but tears of misery.

Luca depressed the accelerator. Shot off along the autostrada heading back to Milan. He was keen to get things moving. He wanted no delays. The wedding would take place as soon as it could be organised.

Personally, he would have been content with a swift civil service, but that was not what his bride would want. Nor Tomaso. So it would be a lavish church wedding, the whole event to be handed over to professionals along with a sky-high budget.

As discussed with Tomaso before he'd left the *palazzo*, it would take place in the beautiful medieval church in the nearby historic town. A picture-book setting that would show off his bride's shy beauty to perfection.

He gave a flickering smile of pleasure and his expression softened. How amazing it was for him to have found her as he had! Her angelic looks were matched by the sweetness of her disposition! Her shy smile…the cerulean blue eyes that looked so tremulously at him…her low, diffident voice. No wonder he'd been instantly smitten. She was everything he'd ever dreamed of—the perfect wife for him!

And, of course, Tomaso Castellani had welcomed his suit. Luca had made it abundantly clear to him that his precious granddaughter would be safe in his oh-so-devoted hands. That she would be as precious to him as to Tomaso, as protected and sheltered as she had been all her life.

'I'll take absolute care of her!' he'd promised, and he would keep that promise. *'Because she deserves it! She is as lovely in her nature as she is in her beauty!'*

There would never be any dissent between them—never any cause for concern, never any disagreement.

She will be my peace...

He could not wait to make her his bride. His wife.

Frustration bit at Ariana as she seized Mia's hands, sitting beside her on the stone bench of the gazebo.

'Just *tell* him! Tell him you don't want to marry him after all!'

Her cousin's face buckled. 'I can't! I *can't*!'

'But why not?' Ariana demanded. 'He's not a monster, is he?'

'No! Of course not! But… But he's…he's so…so *keen*…on me. I can't refuse him! Not after I've already said yes to him!'

Frustration mounted in Ariana, and she had to bite back her instinct to say, *Well, you should never have said yes in the first place then!* Instead she tried another tactic.

'Tell him you were overwhelmed! That it was so sudden, so unexpected, you didn't sufficiently take on board what was happening. Say that he rushed you!'

Her lips pressed tightly. 'Rushed' was an understatement—Mia had known the man less than two months and had spent very little time with him, nearly always in her grandfather's company. OK, so the man had been instantly smitten—given her cousin's exquisite beauty, Ariana could understand that! But surely he would see that Mia needed time—courtship, even—and that marriage was far too important to be rushed?

Didn't her own mother's sorry experience bear witness to that? Running off with her wastrel father and then promptly bolting with a replacement. And then a replacement for the replacement…

She realised her cousin was shaking her head, felt her grip on her hands tightening.

'I *can't*! Oh, Ariana, I'm not outspoken like you are! I can't tell him anything like that! He wants the wedding to be as soon as possible—he doesn't want a long engagement!'

'And what about what *you* want?' Ariana countered, her face working. 'Mia, you don't have to do what others want all the time!' She took a heavy breath. 'Talk to our grandfather! Tell him you don't want to marry! That you feel hustled into it!'

Mia's eyes filled with horror. 'No! That would be even worse! I can't! He's thrilled for me! Overjoyed! I can't do it to him—I can't!'

Ariana squeezed her cousin's limp hands. 'Mia, this is your *life*! You *cannot* marry a man you don't want to marry just because you don't want to reject him, and least of all because you don't want to upset our grandfather! You *have* to stand up for yourself!'

Even as she said that she knew how hopeless it was. Mia had never stood up for herself in her life. Up till now she'd never wanted to—had been content enough, so it seemed, to be their grandfather's favoured grandchild, fussed over and pampered and made much of. All that favouritism had never spoilt Mia, though—she remained as sweet-natured as she always had been.

Too sweet-natured…

She got all the honey and I got all the vinegar, Ariana thought ruefully.

She let Mia's crushed hands go. The thing was, she was just as protective over Mia as their grandfather was. She hated to see her as tearful as she was now.

She got to her feet, looking down at her cousin, her lovely eyes red with crying. There must be a way to extricate her from her predicament. It shouldn't be impossible—after all, Mia was only engaged, and engagements could be broken.

'OK,' Ariana said, sounding brisk and sensible, 'let's think. There must be a way of releasing you without causing anyone any upset.' She looked at Mia a moment, frowning slightly. 'Just to be sure—you *really* don't want to marry this man? I mean, this isn't just nerves, is it? Are you not even a tiny bit in love with him? I mean, if it's got to the point of him proposing…?'

Mia shook her head. 'I'm not in love with him at all!' she exclaimed.

Her gaze slipped past Ariana and she looked out over the gardens through the open shutters of the gazebo. There had been an odd note in Mia's voice. Adamant and evasive.

'Mia? Is there something you're not telling me?' she asked slowly.

She put a hand on her cousin's shoulder, turning her around to face her again. Mia's eyes were filling with tears again.

Realisation dawned in Ariana. 'Oh, Lord,' she said in a hollow voice. 'There's someone else, isn't there?'

The tears spilled down Mia's pale cheeks. 'Nonno will never let me marry him! Never! He's English—a musician. He plays the guitar and he's been busking here in the town, for tourists—that's how I met him. I stopped to listen on my way to the hairdresser and we got talking, and… Well, we've somehow managed to spend some time together, and… Oh, Ariana, I've fallen in love—I truly have. And so has he, with me. But Nonno doesn't know anything about it. And he'd never approve—never! Matt hasn't any money…'

Ariana felt her heart sink. No, a penniless English musician busking for a living would not be their grandfather's idea of a suitable husband for Mia—not by a million miles.

Mia's voice rang out in anguish. 'And Nonno is so pleased that I am going to marry Luca! He's handsome and eligible and fabulously rich.'

Ice reached Ariana's lungs, freezing her breath. Yet through her frozen airway she managed, somehow, to speak.

'Luca…?'

There are many other Lucas—thousands of them! Hundreds of good-looking, incredibly rich ones too... There must be!

But even as she prayed so desperately she heard Mia's answer. The one she knew she would give.

'Yes,' Mia said, getting the words out through her tears. 'Luca Farnese…he's some kind of financier in Milan.'

'Luca Farnese?' Ariana echoed, in a voice like death, and felt every last cell in her body freeze.

CHAPTER FIVE

LUCA WAS IN his office in Milan. He was leaving for Geneva that afternoon, but first he had something quite different from his business affairs to attend to. He pulled the freshly delivered folder on his desk towards him. Its pink and gold delicacy was quite at odds with the dark-grained wood surface. He flicked it open, glancing through the contents so carefully prepared for him by the extremely expensive wedding planner.

Whilst he didn't care about trivia such as floral arrangements and table settings, they would naturally be of interest to his fiancée. A copy had been despatched to her already—he would phone her from Geneva tonight and discuss it with her. Not that Mia would dispute anything—she always went along with everything he wanted without demur. The sweetness of her nature ensured that.

On impulse he picked up his phone, spoke to his PA in the outer office. He would order flowers to be delivered to the *palazzo*. More flowers. And at lunchtime he'd cancel his business appointment and take a look at some of the jewellers in the Galleria Vittorio Emanuele, the famous Milan shopping arcade full of prestigious boutiques. His fiancée already had a massive diamond and sapphire engagement ring, but he would find some pretty trifle for her and have it despatched today.

In his mind he saw her lovely face light up as she opened it. Delight in her celestial blue eyes…

'He keeps sending me things! Flowers every day now—and jewellery! I can't bear it!'

Mia's voice down the telephone was a plaintive wail.

Ariana tensed. Tension was her daily state now—tension and horror. And increasing desperation.

Dear God, Mia *couldn't* marry Luca Farnese! She just couldn't! It was impossible—unthinkable!

I have to stop it somehow...anyhow!

But how? She couldn't get Mia to break it off herself, no matter how hard she tried to persuade her. Nor would Mia go to their grandfather. And she'd almost had hysterics when Ariana had said *she* would tell him.

'No, you can't—you can't! He'll be so angry!' Mia had cried.

The word had tolled like a bell in Ariana's brain. 'Angry' would not be the word if she went to their grandfather and told him the real reason Mia could never marry Luca Farnese…

She shuddered. It was one thing to be defiant against his domestic tyranny—another to see in his face the disgust and the condemnation that would be there if she did tell him. And this time he would have every right to despise her.

Though no one can despise me more than I despise myself for my criminal stupidity.

But if she told Mia, would it give Mia the courage to tell Luca she would not marry him? With a heavy heart, Ariana knew it would not. Nothing would give her gentle, doe-like cousin the courage to do anything she feared to do, anything that would cause upset, make others angry with her…

Claws pincered within Ariana as she finally got Mia off the line. If her cousin would not break her engagement, then only one other person could.

Luca Farnese must break it off.

And, though dread and revulsion filled her, she knew there was only one way to get him to do that.

I have to tell him who Mia is.

Though she would have given a million euros not to have to do so.

Luca snatched up his ringing phone in no good mood. He was back in Milan after a night in Geneva, and to his annoyed disappointment, when he'd phoned the *palazzo* from his hotel to discuss the wedding plans, he'd been informed that his fiancée had retired early. Well, he would try again tonight—and if he needed to he'd drive down the following day to see her in person.

There was the honeymoon to discuss too. He'd already suggested a choice between the Seychelles and the Maldives, and he wanted to settle it. Mia had said she was happy with either, but there was still the resort to be chosen. Somewhere very private—that was his only stipulation.

Very private.

In his mind's eye he could see her…her pale, slender beauty enhanced by the azure waters of the shallow sea, like Botticelli's *Venus*, or the *Venus de Milo*, serene and tranquil. He would lift her into his arms, carry her into their shaded cabana, lay her down upon the waiting bed—

His vision cut out.

The woman had been replaced.

No pale beauty but sultry, dark-eyed, her hair a wanton cloud, her full breasts peaked and straining, her rich mouth lush and parted… She was lying there in his bed, waiting for him. A temptation impossible to resist…

Like a guillotine, he sliced away the forbidden memory.

'What is it?' His snap to his PA, who was calling him, was not civil.

'I am so sorry, Signor Farnese, but this caller is really most insistent. She gives her name as Ariana Killane—' she began.

For a moment that seemed to last for ever blackness filled Luca, obliterating everything else in the universe. Then it cleared.

'Tell Signorina Killane that her services are *not* required,' he said. He drew a sharp breath, indenting his cheeks so that they hollowed starkly. 'She is an interior designer I came across when I was in New York,' he went on, giving his PA an explanation that she could use in future, 'and she has been pestering me since.' His mouth compressed. 'Get rid of her.'

He replaced the phone, stared across the wide office.

Black anger filled him. That she had the temerity to try and contact him *now*, all these weeks later…

Did she not get the message clearly enough? The message that I don't want anything more to do with her.

He sat motionless at his desk. It seemed to him that there was a precipitous drop in front of him. Ready to swallow him up if he did not keep very, very still.

Then he took another breath, slow and deliberate this time, and the sensation eased. His eyes dropped to the pink and white wedding folder. Just seeing it there was reassuring. Soon, in a few brief weeks, his fiancée—his ideal woman—would be his bride. And nothing…*nothing*…was going to stop that.

His eyes darkened. *She* was not going to stop it. The woman he had left behind in New York. The woman he should never have indulged in—who had called him every name under the sun, yelling at him, making a scene…

Memories fused within him. The woman in the bathrobe, yelling at him in front of an elevator. The woman from much longer ago, yelling at his father…

No! He would not allow such memories. Not any more. Never again. They would not, *could* not touch him. He would live his life exactly the way he wanted to, taking total control over everything. Making life do what *he* wanted.

Always.

'Is that Ariana?'

The voice on her mobile was unknown to her, as well as the number calling.

'Yes,' she answered, in the language she'd been addressed in—English. 'Who is this?'

'Matt. I'm Mia's…friend. Look, I'm sorry to phone you, but I don't know what else to do. Mia gave me your number and I… I can't get through to her! She's not answering calls or texts—I'm worried! Really worried!' He paused. 'I'm scared she'll do something stupid.' His voice sounded choked. 'Or already has—'

Chill struck Ariana, but she kept her voice calm. 'OK, Matt. Listen. I'm in Brussels at the moment—at an antiques fair. But I'll phone the *palazzo*, speak to the housekeeper, and ask her to go and check on Mia. Then I'll get right back to you.'

She rang off and did just that. It took for ever to be put through to the housekeeper, and her anxiety only increased while she waited, but when she was finally put through she knew why it had taken so long. And the reason chilled her to the bone.

'Signorina Ariana!' The woman was breathless with agitation. 'Such a scare we've had! But it is all right now. The doctor has been, and Signorina Mia is perfectly well! He has forbidden her to take any more sleeping pills—she must have hot milk and honey, nothing more, if she has insomnia. Your grandfather will insist, so you have nothing to worry about, I promise you. There will not be another such accident.'

Somehow Ariana said what she had to say and rang off. Then she called Matt back, sticking to the housekeeper's interpretation of what had happened. Mia had been confused, forgetting she'd already taken a sleeping pill and taking another one as well…

But what if the overdose hadn't been accidental?

It didn't bear thinking about.

She flew back to Italy early, and drove to the *palazzo*—only to find her cousin not there. Her grandfather had insisted she rest completely, she was told, away from all the wedding preparations, and she had gone to a spa.

'Then I will see my grandfather,' Ariana said grimly.

The maid looked nervous. 'The *signor* is very occupied…' she began.

Ariana ignored her, marching into the library.

The scene that followed was hideous, but she did not flinch from it. Could not.

'You *cannot* let her go through with this wedding—not after this!' she threw at her grandfather. 'Even if it was only an accident…' she would not put into words her greatest fear '…what state of mind must she be in to make such a dangerous mistake? This isn't just pre-wedding nerves. She doesn't want this wedding to happen! You *must* see that!'

She might as well have saved her breath.

Her grandfather surged to his feet, face red with instant rage, banging his stick on the floor in fury. He rang a peal over her head, accusing her of jealousy, of wanting to ruin her cousin's happiness, of causing trouble as she always did!

'And do not think to spread your poison to your cousin directly! I have given orders that you are not to see her. You are not welcome—so get out. Get out!'

Ariana got out, her grandfather's vituperation echoing in her ears as she drove away, heaviness pressing down upon her. The wedding was in a week. What could she possibly, possibly do now to stop it as Mia had begged her to?

It was in the long, sleepless reaches of the night that it came to her. The only way. Unthinkable—but it would achieve what had to be achieved. Ugly, painful, desperate, and it would take every ounce of her nerve and strength of will to carry it out, so repugnant was it to her.

But she would have to do it.

There was no other way.

Somehow she must let her cousin know she would not fail her in her hour of need. However desperate the means…

Luca stood by the altar rail, watching with a softening of his expression as his bride approached on her grandfather's arm. Soon—very soon now—she would be his. And he would devote himself to her…to her happiness.

She will be my life and I will give her everything she wants! Everything she could ever want!

He could see it already in his mind. Their placid life together, peaceful and serene, devoted to each other…

My sweet, gentle Mia...

He smiled warmly at her as Tomaso patted her hand, then placed it on Luca's own. He felt it tremble and was moved by that. Her face was hidden by a long veil, and he was glad of that. The gown was simple, but beautiful, with a demure sweetheart neckline, and the folds of the skirt fell into a graceful train held by pretty little flower girls with wreaths in their hair. He had no idea who they were, nor her maid of honour—relatives, he assumed, or the daughters of friends. He was not concerned with his exquisite bride's family—only with his bride herself.

She was like a fantasy come true…

And just as perfect.

His smile of reassurance deepened. He did not mind that she appeared a little nervous, a little tense—he approved of it, even. Someone as delicate as she *should* feel emotional at her wedding…

He could not see her eyes through the veil, but that did not matter so long as she could see him clearly. He pressed her slender hand, to reassure her once more, and felt it tremble again. Then the priest began the service with a clearing of his throat, and Luca turned his attention to him.

His thoughts were strange as the ceremony progressed. Memories flickered across his mind.

Last night he'd dreamt that he was a young boy again, kneeling by the banister, filled with fear at the angry yelling coming from downstairs as his mother raged at his father, vitriolic and denouncing. And then had come the slamming of a door. And the silence. Deadly, ominous silence. And fear had bitten at his throat like a wolf…

He'd awoken in a cold sweat, and it had taken a while to bring himself entirely out of the dream and realise how different his reality was now. How it always would be.

His eyes went to the quiet, beautiful woman at his side. A line of Shakespeare drifted through his head. *'My gracious silence...'*

Then the priest paused in his sonorous recitation of

the words of the marriage service and Luca frowned, wondering why. What had the man just said?

'If any of you know just cause or impediment…'

Ah, yes, that was it—the infamous *Speak now or for ever hold your peace* bit.

For a second, a moment of time so brief it did not really exist, a memory flashed, so vivid, so intense, it seared like a brand across his skull.

A naked body, lush and wanton, a cloud of hair around a face set with deep smoky eyes, a rich scarlet mouth lifted to his... And desire, hot and humid, searing and urgent, scorching through him.

No! He banished it, obliterated it. Destroyed it utterly. It did not exist. He would not permit it to exist. Would crush it out of existence. It was in the past. Over. Finished as soon as it had happened.

No impediment...

No, none—because he would not allow it. He would allow only what was happening now. He drew a breath. Certainty filled him. No, there was no just cause or impediment whatsoever against him taking the woman of his dreams to be his wife…

Except…

From the back of the church came footsteps—like nails striking the flagstones of the aisle. A voice—harsh and strident—was breaking the hallowed silence. Heads were turning…breaths were being held across the congregation.

A voice was calling out.

Announcing.

Denouncing…

He felt his head turn. Felt his gaze falling on the figure of the woman walking down the aisle. A red suit exposed every curve of her voluptuous body. A matching pill box hat with a black veil concealed her face.

A veil she threw back as she approached.

At his side he heard Tomaso give a snarl of rage, start forward.

But he himself did not move. Could not.

He could only level his eyes on her with a fury he had not known he could possess—a fury that should strike her into silence if there were any justice in the world… any decency.

But there was no justice…no decency. There was only her voice, ringing out like sacrilege. Freezing him to the very marrow of his bones.

'He *cannot* marry her!' she cried out. 'I am pregnant with his child!'

The whole world had frozen. *She* had frozen. Ariana's hand dropped to her side, suddenly as heavy as lead. In front of her she could see the appalling tableau—her grandfather clutching his silver-topped stick, then raising it as if he would lunge forward and strike her. Luca standing there, as frozen as she, his eyes like pits, basilisk in their power to destroy her. And Mia—whose slight, slender body suddenly buckled…

Instinctively, Ariana lurched forward to try to catch her, but her cousin's bridegroom was there before her, folding her against him to stop her fainting fall. She saw her grandfather's stick clatter to the flagstones and then he was beside Mia as well, the priest too, helping her to a pew. Everyone was gathering around her. All across the church voices were raised…people were aghast, appalled.

Ariana turned. Fled. Filled with sickness and horror at what she had done. What she had had to do…been forced to do…

Because there was no other way...no other way...no other way...

The words screamed in her head, circling like angry seagulls, shrieking and flapping.

She burst out of the church, desperate to get away, to find her car. It was parked in the next street, for the *piazza* had been kept clear for the wedding cars.

The bright sunshine blinded her—or something did. But she gained the edge of the *piazza*, saw her car pulled up against the pavement, one of many parked there by the guests. Urgently she fumbled for her keys, pressing the button to unlock, yanking open the driver's door.

An oath sounded behind her, running feet. Her arm was seized, her body hauled around.

Luca, his face black with fury, his hand closing over her other arm, was shaking her as if she were a rag held in his iron grip.

'How *dare* you?' he snarled. 'I will *destroy* you for what you did!'

Fury filled him—a rage so black it was flooding his veins, blinding his vision. But it was not obliterating the face of the woman who had done what she had just done.

'You vicious, jealous, destructive *witch*!'

He shook her again, as if he could make her disintegrate before his eyes.

But she was throwing her head back.

'I tried to talk to you! I *tried*! You wouldn't let me! There was nothing else I could do—'

The words were falling from her, defensive, vehement. Her eyes were distending, her face contorted.

He heard her take a ragged breath, plunge on.

'You wouldn't let me talk to you—warn you—'

'*Warn* me?'

Fury flooded him again. His mouth twisted derisively. He saw her face blench and was glad of it. Savagely glad.

'Warn me that you were so twisted and vicious that you would think nothing of destroying the wedding day of a completely innocent woman! Hurl at me a monstrous *lie*!' His mouth twisted. 'You're no more pregnant than a nun! I damn well used protection—'

His hands dropped away. To touch her, even in anger, was to taint him.

His eyes scored hers. 'Well?' he demanded, and there was ice in his voice now, not fury. 'Are you pregnant? Tell me to my face.'

Slowly, he saw her shake her head, and he felt again that fury engorge in his throat. His mouth twisted and he stepped away. It was not safe for him to be this close to her…

'Get out,' he said softly. It was a softness that he saw made her blench again. 'Get out. And if you *ever* come near my bride again, I'll—'

She gave a cry, throwing herself into the driver's seat,

slamming the door shut, but opening the window. 'You *can't* marry her now! You *can't*!'

He leant forward, menace in every line of his body. 'I will do,' he said, 'exactly what I wish. I will tell her you were lying through your teeth in your despicable claim!'

'No! You *won't*! Because Mia is my *cousin*—and if you *dare* to think of marrying her now I will tell her what happened in New York! She will *never* marry you then! *Never!*'

He heard her fire the ignition, the throaty roar of the powerful engine silencing everything except the shock slicing across his brain. She shot off into the narrow cobbled street and he watched her go.

There was blackness in his soul.

And deadly, deadly rage.

Ariana was in her apartment over her office and showroom in a fashionable street in Lucca. She was staring at the text Mia had sent. It was simple, and brief.

Thank you with all my heart.

She felt sick.

Shakily, she flicked off the screen, dropping the phone on her bedside table. She was in a dressing gown, her hair wet around her shoulders. She'd been in the shower for half an hour, as if she might sluice from her body the memory of what she'd done that day. What she'd *had* to do.

Scandal, outrage—lies.

That showstopping lie in front of all the world to

halt the wedding ceremony, to give Mia the chance she needed to escape her fate, to let her cousin faint dramatically to make it stop. Just make it *stop.*

And the other desperate lie—the one she had hurled at Luca Farnese, inverting the truth, desperate that he should believe it. Believe that Mia, who had been unable to face telling him she didn't want to marry him, would denounce him for having slept with her cousin…

She gave a choking sob. Only one person would be doing any denouncing. Her grandfather. And it would not be Luca Farnese he denounced.

She would take the fall for what she had done. She and she alone. For ruining Mia's wedding…for halting it in its tracks…for making it impossible for it to take place.

Well, she had succeeded in that—outrageous and drastic as her method had been. Had had to be.

And now… She shut her eyes, weary beyond anything in the aftermath of what she had done. Now there was just her life to get on with.

Her ordeal was finally over, and that, at least, was something to be grateful for.

Her grandfather would never speak to her again—but then how great a loss would that be? She had been condemned in his eyes long ago, by the very fact of her birth. This was only the finish of it.

As for Mia—well, she was free. And if she could find some way to elope with her beloved Matt…if she could somehow find the courage to do so…

I'll help her financially—I can afford it.

Wearily, she climbed into bed. She could sleep for

a week after all the horrors of the day. So long as she did not dream.

Did not dream of the fury in Luca's eyes. The hatred in them. The loathing.

She gave another sob, pulling the bedclothes over her damp, tangled hair. Seeking the blessed oblivion of sleep…

CHAPTER SIX

LUCA REPLACED THE phone on his desk, a look of grim satisfaction on his face at what his lawyer had told him. Never had his features appeared so aquiline—he looked like a bird of prey, circling silently above its intended victim grazing unaware below.

Ariana Killane would pay for what she had done in that hideous, ugly scene at the wedding. And not just done to himself. To a victim completely innocent of anything. Mia—the sweet, gentle bride he'd longed for all his life—had done *nothing* to deserve what had been done to her that nightmare day. She'd even fainted with the shock, the horror of it all, on her very wedding day…

Done to her by her own cousin.

The fact that Ariana Killane was the cousin of the woman he'd wanted to marry was still unbearable to him. It had been thrown at him with such vicious spite, utterly destroying any chance of winning back his bride. How he could possibly marry Mia now, having taken her cousin to bed first?

She would hold me in revulsion—and rightly so!

He felt his guts hollow with self-loathing at what he

had done that disastrous night in New York. That night he should never have indulged in, which had reached its tentacles across an entire ocean to entangle him here. Meshing him tight. Destroying the marriage he could now never make.

Impossible to try and redeem the situation.

Only to level retribution upon the woman who had done this to him.

Destroy her life as she had destroyed his.

Ariana was in the office that opened off the stylish showroom she rented to show off selected pieces of furniture and artfully draped fabrics, as well as lamps, rugs and assorted *objets d'art* which might tempt potential clients to come in and book her services. She was going through her post, doggedly letting herself focus only on the usual mix of invoices and supplier notes, fabric samples, cheques and business correspondence, blocking her mind to anything else.

It was the only way to keep going—not thinking, not remembering, not replaying on an endless loop that nightmare day of Mia's wedding two endless, punishing weeks ago. It was over. It was done. That was what she had to keep saying to herself.

As for Luca Farnese…

She felt a chill inside her—and something more. Something that was like a cry of pain. The hatred in his face, the rage—the loathing… The memory was like knives stabbing her. Agonising.

Why? Why should it hurt that he hates me so much for what I did at his wedding? The wedding he deserted me for in New York...the wedding that he had intended to go through with even before he laid eyes on me! A man so despicable—to take another woman to bed with a bride waiting for him in Italy! But didn't I know what he was that morning I woke up without him? Didn't I know from that very moment what he was capable of?

She stared blindly at the next envelope in her in tray. It was marked 'Private and Confidential' and addressed to her personally, not to her business. She reached for her paper knife, sliced open the envelope, took out the typed letter within. It was from a firm of lawyers she had never heard of.

And as her eyes scanned the page she realised, with a sickening clench of her guts, just what Luca Farnese was indeed capable of…

'Signorina Killane, he accuses you of defaming him in a public place. That is the basis for his claim. He says you made a scurrilous accusation, knowing it was untrue, exposing him to the vilification and obloquy of all who heard you, materially damaging his reputation. You acted, so he maintains, out of malice and spite, ruining his wedding—a wedding upon which a great deal of money had been spent—humiliating him and alienating his bride, with the intention of revenging yourself for his perceived scorning of you following a highly transient sexual liaison of no duration and no emotional or personal significance whatsoever.'

The middle-aged bespectacled man addressing her across his desk steepled his hands, glancing down at the letter Ariana had shakily given to him, full of legal jargon, which he had just read. He shook his head.

'He is attempting to seek remedy in law,' he told her soberly.

'What can I do?' The words fell fearfully from Ariana's lips.

Her lawyer pressed his lips together and took a breath. 'Going to court is expensive, and you would run the risk not only of having to pay the damages he is seeking, but his legal costs as well as your own. I can only recommend attempting to settle with him out of court—as is set out here.'

'But he is demanding a fortune!' Ariana closed her eyes. The very air seemed to be choking her, as if it were toxic to breathe. 'I can't afford that sum,' she said. 'It would financially cripple me. Wipe me out.'

'Perhaps your grandfather—?' began her lawyer.

Her eyes flashed open. 'He'd see me starve in the gutter before he lifted a finger to help me!'

She got to her feet, her body as heavy as lead. 'I'll go to see my accountants—see if they can advise anything.'

That was indeed her next port of call, but she came away as dead in the water as she had feared. A loan of that magnitude…? Against her business…? Her accountant had shaken his head dolefully, saying he would do what he could but was not hopeful.

Bitterly, she made her way back to her elegant shop, walked into her office, sat down at her desk. She stared into space. There was a stone inside her. A boulder.

It would all go. Everything she had spent her adult life building up. Everything she had striven for, day after day, taking such pride and satisfaction in the fact that she was, by her own efforts, her own skills, gaining her independence from her grandfather, escaping his hold over her.

She set her face. Took a heavy, painful breath. Well, there was one thing at least she could be glad of. Matt and Mia were together.

After fainting at the wedding, Mia had been whisked off by their grandfather in a state of complete collapse to a private clinic, to recover from her ordeal and the ruination of her intended marriage. Ariana, of course, had been allowed no communication with her at all.

But she had stayed in touch with Matt, and had made over to him a sizeable sum of money that would enable him to launch his music career in London and rent accommodation there for himself and Mia, supporting them both. The next she'd heard Mia had discharged herself from the clinic and headed for London with Matt, planning to marry him the moment she could.

So at least what I did for Mia was worthwhile...

It was the only comfort afforded to her. Now she sat her desk, facing the ruin of everything she'd worked so hard to build for herself. All that was left was to wait for the axe to fall. Wielded by Luca Farnese. His killing blow.

In her head she heard his voice, black with savage fury. *'I will destroy you.'*

He would do so, she knew, without mercy or compunction. For what she had done to him.

Luca sat at his desk, an expression of grim satisfaction once more on his face. Now to spring the trap. The trap he'd set by issuing the writ for defamation, to which Ariana had responded in exactly the way he'd anticipated. She wouldn't risk a court case—she'd settle, just as her lawyer had informed his own.

Now it was time to contact her accountant. The man who was trying to find her a loan of sufficient magnitude to enable her to settle out of court.

Well, he was a magnanimous man—there was a limit to how much justice he would exact on Ariana Killane and what form it would take. He'd been the hard man with her. Now it was time for the softer approach. The generous gesture.

He smiled, picking up his phone. It was not a pleasant smile. Not pleasant at all.

Ariana's eyes widened.

'Are you *sure*?' she queried.

Her accountant repeated what he'd just told her and her grip on her phone tightened. Could it be true? Had he really found a loan for her?

Fort the first time since that dreadful day of Mia's abortive wedding, three weeks ago, Ariana felt hope returning. She listened avidly as her accountant ran through the conditions. They were tough, with the interest rate high, the term short, but if she could keep her turnover going, could sustain her profit margins, then, yes, she might—just might—be able to stay in business, get clear of debt eventually, and emerge intact. She'd been warned that the loan was repayable on demand, but why would the lender do that if she made her repayments on schedule? Besides, without this loan she would go under anyway.

But I'll fight to save myself! Save everything I've worked for! I'll work every hour God sends!

'So, you are happy for me to proceed and give agreement?' her accountant was checking now.

'Yes! Oh, definitely, definitely yes!' she exclaimed immediately.

Ten minutes later, with the loan agreement signed by her digitally, it was done. Hanging up, she felt as if a crushing weight had been lifted from her.

As if to prove the stars were smiling on her, her mobile pinged. It was Mia.

'Ariana—darling Ariana! I couldn't wait to tell you! Matt's hired a recording studio! It's all set up, and it's all thanks to you! And we've got a date for the wedding! Please, please come—it will mean everything to us after all you've done!' Her voice changed. 'Are you quite sure you can afford all the money you've given us?'

'Of course I can!' Ariana lied immediately.

Gladness filled her as Mia chattered happily. Whether or not Matt ever found fame and fortune, he and Mia would be happy, for he was the man her cousin loved. And Mia was the woman Matt loved.

Her expression faltered a moment when Mia finally rang off. Mia, so sweet-natured, so angelic… Was it any surprise that Luca, too, had fallen for her?

The way he never fell for me.

Into her head stabbed Luca's harsh, scathing accusation. *'Jealous—vindictive.'*

Her face contorted. Was he right? Was she jealous

of Mia and wanting to punish the man who had made it brutally clear that all Ariana had been was a meaningless one-night stand? Someone merely to slake a passing, momentary lust and nothing more than that? She pushed the thoughts from her head.

Luca's callous rejection of her was *not* the reason she had sought to stop him marrying her cousin! It wasn't!

I did it for Mia! Only for her!

The sound of the showroom door opening as someone came in stopped her self-tormenting inquisition, silenced the memory of Luca's condemnation. Getting up from her desk, she walked through from her office, putting a professional smile on her face for whoever had come in, whether it was just to browse or to make enquiries about her interior design services. Services she was now under desperate pressure to sell to as many clients as possible, if she were to have any chance of survival at all…

But as she walked in, without any premonition at all, she stopped dead.

The smile died on her face.

It was Luca Farnese standing there.

Luca saw the smile wiped from Ariana's face, and his eyes glittered. Hers widened in shock. Horror.

'You!'

The word shot like a bullet from her and a hand shot out to grab the door frame, as if to stop herself reeling back. Her other hand flew up in a gesture so automatically defensive he could have laughed. But his humour was tightly leashed—and so much else beside.

Calmly, he helped himself to the chair set in front of

the elegant antique desk where clients could sit and discuss their requirements, crossing one long leg casually over the other and looking across at the woman standing framed in the doorway. He leashed his emotions tighter.

She'd gone pale as whey—the way she had when he'd confronted her by her car in the *piazza* outside the church, trying to flee the scene of her crime. The knuckles of the hand gripping the door frame were as white as her face, the nails as scarlet as her lush lips, parting now in the expression of horror crossing her face.

'I thought you might like to know the source of the loan you've just accepted,' he opened, enjoying every moment of this meeting with a savage sense of pleasure at what he was about to inflict upon her.

Justice, meet and fitting, for what she had done, the lives she had ruined—his and her innocent victim's… her own cousin! She'd had neither pity nor regard for her, callously and deliberately humiliating her in the worst possible way at her own wedding.

She seemed to sway, and in her distended eyes he saw realisation. The realisation that it was he, all along, sufficiently disguised through intermediaries, who had offered her the oh-so-convenient and timely lifeline of the loan that she had clutched at so eagerly. Given her binding signature to.

Giving herself into his power.

He smiled. She was not slow to understand—he'd give her that. Nor to cut to the chase.

'Why?'

She whispered the single word, and he answered it succinctly.

'You cost me my bride,' he told her. 'And you ruined your cousin's future. A cousin who had done *nothing* to earn your spite and malice.'

His tone was impersonal. He might as well be making some comment about the weather. He smoothed the material of his trouser leg, looking up at her again.

'But, unlike you, I'm not vindictive. I threatened to sue you for defamation precisely to get you to this point—borrowing money from me via a shell finance company I happen to own. You will pay the financial damages due to me. But,' he added silkily, 'there are other ways to pay damages that are not financial.'

He looked about him. The showroom held an ultra-tasteful display of expensive wares likely to induce wealthy women to wander in…perhaps to purchase some of them, perhaps to consider engaging Ariana Killane to refresh their assorted residences, either in Italy or further afield.

Memory plucked at him, of her telling him about it over that fateful dinner in Manhattan, when he'd crushed all his misgivings, ignored his knifing consciousness that had told him succumbing to the temptation he was indulging in would be a bad, bad mistake…

He pushed the memory aside—it served no purpose. There was only one purpose in him now: to exact his retribution from the woman who had taken from him the future he'd thought was within his grasp.

He heard his own accusation replay in his head. *'You cost me my bride.'*

His mouth tightened into a whipped line. His bride, the woman of his dreams—gentle, ethereally beautiful Mia, with her sweet nature and her quiet, tranquil ways—was lost to him. All that was left to him was this woman who had brought about that loss.

A woman who thought nothing of others. Who could spew vitriolic abuse in front of a crowded elevator and not care who saw or heard her histrionics. Who could play out her egotistical diva dramatics in the middle of a church, the middle of a wedding ceremony, leaving shockwaves echoing and the congregation aghast at the appalling scene, her aged grandfather near apoplectic and her own cousin collapsing in horror at the lie she'd hurled at her.

Well, Ariana Killane would pay for what she'd done to her own cousin, and to himself. He would destroy the business she valued so much in a fitting retribution.

But there was something else he was going to destroy too. His eyes glittered with dark intent. It wasn't just Ariana's business he would break. He was going to break her power over him—the power that had made him commit his greatest folly and cost him the future he'd dreamt of all his life.

I will break it because I must.

Because if he didn't…

His eyes fastened on her, standing there, still frozen, still ashen, her face stricken with shock and hollowing dismay.

He could feel his body's reaction to her despite his iron self-control, despite her white face. Her rich, sensual beauty blazed in his vision.

She was wearing a business suit in a deep royal blue, cinched at the waist, lapels curving over her full breasts, the skirt easing over her rounded hips, tight around her shapely thighs…thighs his hands had stroked, caressed, parted with his questing touch. The long, waving hair through which his fingers had sifted so lusciously that disastrous night in Manhattan was caught back now, confined in a net snood that begged to be ripped from her in order to let loose its glorious tresses, a living waterfall over her naked back and engorged breasts… Just as that confining, clinging suit begged to be stripped from her, to reveal the irresistible curves of her willing, wanton body…

But resist he must.

His jaw set, taut with effort, he veiled his gaze with equal effort. Resist he *would*… He would break her power over him. And break her as he did so.

Time to complete his retribution.

His gaze flicked over her. Still veiled.

'Tell me,' he said, resting his eyes impassively on her pale face, 'how long do you think it will take you to repay the loan you have just taken out to cover my claim for damages? I set the interest rate high, so you must take that into account. Given your current turnover—and, yes, I have a full dossier on you now…it was a condition I demanded of your accountant before I agreed the loan—and given your lack of assets to realise other than your stock… I am aware that this property is leased—that you do not own the freehold and nor do you own any other property. I would calculate it will take you five years at the earliest to be completely free of the principal of the loan I have made you.'

He was watching her face but her expression did not

change, nor her skin's pallor. She stood there, immobile, knuckles still white, her free hand still raised as if to ward him off. Yet he could see, with satisfaction, that it had begun to tremble. It was as imperceptible as her shallow breathing but she was under stress. Extreme stress. He was glad of it. She deserved no less.

He waited, but she made no answer. After a moment, letting his words sink into her, he decided to continue. He had issued the bad news. Now he would feed her the good news.

But it will not prove good for her...

He felt his mouth tighten, his muscles steel, and deliberately relaxed his body, easing it back in the chair, never for an instant taking his eyes from her.

'Five years…' he echoed, musingly. 'Five years of being in my debt. Five long, punishing years. If, of course, I don't choose to call in the debt before then—I'm sure you understand that was one of the conditions I set.'

He took a breath, a considered intake of air, his gaze on her like a basilisk.

'But, as I said, there are other ways, Ariana.' His voice was gentle. 'Other ways to be free of debt.'

She did not move—not an iota. But the trembling in her upraised frozen hand was now discernible. Still she did not speak. So he spelt it out for her.

'You see,' he said, and his tone was nothing more than conversational, his gaze on her expressionless, 'you have ensured that Mia is lost to me for ever. So, since I cannot have the wife of my choice, I have decided to make do…' he smiled, the merest parting of his lips over his teeth '…with a mistress.'

He paused, savouring the moment. Savouring the flaring in her eyes…what it meant. His own eyes flickered over her again, and then met hers, head-on.

He went for the kill. 'You auditioned very well, Ariana—New York proved that quite adequately.'

He saw her eyes shut, then open again. Saw her whole body recoil, like a snake rearing to strike.

'Go to hell,' she said. Her words were ground from her, her mouth barely moving.

He shook his head. 'No, I don't think so. I want something out of this…this debacle. Something other than mere money, of which I have plenty. The loan itself is paltry—well, to me, at least. And besides, why should you object? You fell into bed with me the first time easily enough—and you enjoyed it considerably, to my recollection. So why not again? And besides,' he added, enjoying this moment too, 'this time around there will be an added bonus for you.' He paused. Then, 'If you please me sufficiently,' he said consideringly, 'I may make the loan a gift instead.' He got to his feet. 'Think it over,' he said. 'Then have dinner with me tonight.'

He gave her the name of his hotel and took his leave.

Only as he turned at her showroom door to take one last look at her did he feel something clench inside him, as if steel claws had sprung a trap. Which was strange, really—since it was he who'd sprung his trap on her. But the steel claws inside him clenched tighter, as if closing over flesh.

His own flesh.

* * *

Ariana dressed with care. A dark blue evening gown, sleeveless, high under her breasts, with a scooped yoke set with steel coloured beading, narrow skirts falling to her ankles. She wore it with a loose-fitting evening jacket in a filmy material, an even darker shade of blue, that skimmed her arms in batwing sleeves. She wore her hair up, in a pompadour style to give her extra height, along with four-inch satin evening shoes. Every centimetre helped.

She studied her reflection in the cheval glass in her bedroom, remembering, with a wash of nausea, how she'd sat at that vanity unit in the restroom of the Manhattan hotel, wondering if she'd put on too much make-up, worn too tight a dress.

Would it have made a difference if she hadn't? What if she simply hadn't gone to Marnie van Huren's party at all? If she'd made a polite excuse and gone for an early night instead?

So many chances to avoid this moment now, as she stood staring at herself in the long glass, wondering how she had come to this point.

And one chance above all.

She saw herself again, leaving that hotel in Manhattan, saw Luca Farnese turning to her.

'Have dinner with me.'

She felt her throat thicken. All she'd had to do was shake her head demurringly, murmur, *Thank you, but no.* And this moment would never have come.

But she hadn't. And it had.

And now all she could do was this: pick up her evening bag and leave her bedroom, walk out of her apartment on to the pavement below, get into the waiting taxi. Give the driver the name of the hotel.

Luca Farnese's hotel. Where he was waiting for her. Waiting to make her his mistress.

She felt emotion writhe within her, twisting like a snake. She silenced it, crushed it. She must not allow it. Must allow no emotion at all.

There was one purpose to this evening and one only.

Survival.

CHAPTER SEVEN

LUCA WAS IN his hotel suite, pacing up and down. He was not usually restless, and he tried to contain it now. But he could not be still. His mind was too agitated. The absolute self-control he'd exerted over himself that afternoon had taxed him to the limit.

With an effort of sheer will he stopped pacing. Looked about him. The reception room of the suite served as both sitting and dining room, and the table was set for dining.

Intimate dining.

Memory slashed at him…dining in that Manhattan restaurant with her. The woman he'd walked away with from that party, having had no such intention at all. His words inviting her to dinner—to so much more than dinner—had been out of his mouth before he'd been able to stop them or even want to stop them. And from that moment on—from the moment of her consent to let him take her to dine—the rest of her consent had been a given. Not once had she said no to him.

She wanted everything—everything that happened! Gave herself to it—could not get enough of it.

All night long.

It was like a wall crumbling. A wall he'd erected, brick by punishing brick, ever since he'd stood in the early morning in that Manhattan hotel room, looking down at her sleeping form, her hair tousled across the pillow, her body exhausted from their congress…her voluptuous, sensual body.

He knew every silken centimetre of it—had felt it shuddering beneath his, arching like a bow, straining every fibre, spread-eagled for his possession again and again and again… He had gazed down on it, knowing that he must leave her, whatever it took, whatever it cost. He must walk out.

Walk out and claim the woman he had left behind in Italy. The woman who had been lost to him now. Taken from him.

Now all that was left to him was to inflict his retribution on the woman who had cost him his bride—cost him so much more.

But *never again* would she have the power to do so. Not after tonight. Tonight would finish it. It *must.*

He felt emotion, powerful and raw, scythe within him. Blackness filled the dark sockets of his eyes.

Ariana walked up to the reception desk at the ultra-elegant boutique hotel, converted from a wealthy merchant's house in the *centro storico.*

'Signor Farnese,' she murmured.

Her head was high, her spine straight. She would do this in style. Whatever the depths of her humiliation.

The lift swept her up, and as she stepped out she saw

the door to the suite opposite was already open—the clerk must have phoned through to announce her arrival. She could almost hear her heart beating, as if a bird were trapped inside her. One whose wings could never break free of its prison.

She walked inside, taking in the antique furniture, the floral display on a marquetry pier table. The only modern touch was a pair of sofas either side of a coffee table, on which was a bottle of champagne and two flutes.

But her eyes went only to the man standing by the window, open to the warm air of early summer. The man who was going to destroy her. Who already had.

Unless…

She felt emotion bite in her throat, bitter as gall. Poisoning her.

But she would not let him know. That, alone, would be her only salvation now.

'Champagne?' Luca made his invitation laconic.

'Why not?' came the equally laconic reply.

Ariana Killane strolled forward, approaching the coffee table, and picked up one of the empty flutes, a nonchalant air about her.

The flicker of a sardonic smile played around Luca's mouth. So that was how she was going to present herself—as if none of this mattered to her. Well, he would let her play it that way—for the time being.

His eyes rested on her. She looked magnificent. Appreciation purred inside him. Succumbing to her seductive allure in New York had been madness—every sane particle of his brain had told him so, even while his body had been inflamed by her, wanting only to possess her, to slake itself in her, in his searing desire for her.

But now—now it was very different. He would prove he was master of himself. Permit her no power over him. Only he had the power. And he would use it to the full.

He kept his eyes fixed on her as he opened the champagne bottle, filling both glasses. 'What shall we drink to?' he murmured, his eyes never leaving hers. It was a taunt, and he knew it—and so did she.

She didn't answer, and he knew she wouldn't—her veneer of civility was rice-paper-thin, and he could see her tension in the line of her mouth, betraying the indifference she was feigning.

'Then I think that to an enjoyable evening is appropriate, don't you?' Luca posed the question with a lift of one eyebrow.

Again, she didn't answer. Her mouth only tightened minutely. In her eyes, deep in their smoky depths, he saw daggers… Swiftly sheathed, the blades concealed.

They only amused him. She had no power to strike him. He would grant her none. Never again.

He took a draught of the softly fizzing champagne, savouring its bouquet, watching her as she did the same, but taking only a small sip, as if it might choke her to drink more.

He lowered his glass, gesturing around the suite with his hand. He would select an innocuous topic to converse on, knowing it was as meaningless as their superficial civility towards each other. But it would serve his purpose all the same. Pass the time until he made his move on her. Broke her power over him.

'So, from your professional point of view, what do you make of this hotel?' he invited. It was an open question, posed in a socially inviting voice, deliberately so.

Was she grateful for such a neutral topic of conversation? Her expression gave nothing away. The mask she was wearing over that flawless face was perfect—except for that tell-tale tension in the set of her mouth, and the dark daggers in the depths of her eyes.

'It's been excellently and expertly done,' she said. Her tone of voice matched her air of cultivated indifference towards the reason she was here.

'Not one of your interiors, though?'

He spoke as if her answer might possibly interest him, but knew she saw through it when she merely said, 'I don't do commercial work.'

Luca took another leisurely mouthful of champagne. 'And how is your business looking?' His smile was thin, his voice barely concealing the taunt. 'You will appreciate that I now have a vested interest in your turnover and profits.'

Memory snapped in him, of how he'd asked her what her turnover was that evening over dinner in Manhattan, and how she'd drawn back from his enquiry. Now she had no option but to tell him.

She did so coolly, in a crisp, businesslike fashion, outlining progress on current projects, indicating other prospects not yet confirmed, detailing upcoming costs, incoming payments. She answered all his questions fluently, holding her own under his probing interrogation.

Out of nowhere he found himself contrasting her to

the woman he had intended to marry. What had he ever talked to Mia about?

Our wedding, mostly, and assuring her that although we would live in Milan we would make extended visits to the grandfather she's devoted to.

But what else had they talked about? He could not recall. Only that she had seldom said much.

But her quietness was what I craved.

He steered his thoughts away. Mia was lost to him. Taken from him by her own cousin's spite.

His eyes rested on Ariana, who was answering some question he'd put to her about the current stock value of the inventory she was carrying, and he heard himself interrupt her. 'Have you always been jealous of your cousin?'

Her expression changed. Closed like a door shutting him out.

'Mia is not a subject I am prepared to discuss,' she said. Her voice was clipped.

A stab of anger smote Luca. 'You ruin her life and presume to say that? To *me*, of all people?'

But her face remained closed, mouth set. 'I won't talk about her,' she repeated. 'What happened in New York made your marriage to her impossible. You wouldn't let me near you to warn you—'

His hand shot up. *'Basta!'* He would not tolerate her accusation! Her attempt to justify what she had done. The hideous debacle she had caused without a thought for her cousin—for how her words had caused Mia to collapse into a faint, prostrate with shock and dismay…

He took a heavy breath. He'd been a fool to turn the

conversation to what she'd done. What did it matter that she sought to justify herself? It was impossible for her to do so. Her behaviour towards Mia was beyond contempt…

He fought for composure again and slammed down the emotions leaping within him. The anger she made him feel. He reached for the champagne bottle, refilling his own flute and hers without asking her. Then, crossing to the house phone, he gave the order for dinner to be served.

It came quickly, and he was glad. The serving of it gave him time to calm himself, get back in control. The control it was essential for him to exert to make her destruction complete.

How she got through dinner Ariana didn't know. She ate mechanically, which was an abuse of the gourmet dishes placed in front of her, grateful that the serving staff had not been dismissed. It gave her some shelter—frail but at least present—from being alone with Luca Farnese. The man who had summoned her here to spend the night with him.

While the waiting staff were there he kept up a flow of small talk, to which she replied as mechanically as she ate. What it was about she had little idea—Lucca, mostly, and its history…the annual opera festival held in honour of its most famous son, Giacomo Puccini. She hardly knew. Or cared. All her strength was going into staying seated, lifting her fork to her mouth, making whatever replies were appropriate.

Not looking at him.

Not remembering.

As the excruciating meal finally finished, and she pushed aside her half-eaten *tarte framboise*, she heard Luca speak to the staff, telling them to serve coffee in the sitting area of the suite. Then he got to his feet.

'Shall we?' he said to Ariana.

His voice was smooth. Too smooth.

She stood up too, and walked across to one of the pair of facing sofas, sitting down on it with as much poise as she could muster, feeling the folds of her dress drape softly on the velvet upholstery. She had drunk very little wine, yet along with the glass of champagne earlier it had been more than dangerous. She could feel her heart rate increase, the tension racking through her.

Soon, very soon now, she would face her fate.

She watched the serving staff set out a coffee tray in front of her and clear away the dinner dishes, saw Luca presenting them with an obviously generous tip before they wheeled away the trolleys.

Leaving her alone with Luca Farnese.

And all that must shortly come.

The dread thudding in her heart grew heavier yet.

He sat down on the sofa opposite her. Without volition her eyes went to him. Went to his aquiline profile as he leant forward slightly to pour coffee, the expensive material of his dark grey suit straining across his powerful thighs. Thighs that had pressed her oh-so-yielding body into the mattress that unforgettable night in New York…

Her eyes went to his hands now, as his long, strong fingers curved around the silver coffee pot handle—hands that had stroked her body, fingers that had expertly caressed her body's innermost secret recesses, drawn from her a shuddering ecstasy that had made her cry out aloud in gasping breaths her neck and spine arched impossibly.

She remembered her own hands digging into the supple sinews of his broad muscled shoulders as he brought her to a peak of pleasure that she had never known… only to realise she had not even begun to feel all he could make her feel as her body bowed, lifting for him, and he plunged deep within her in total, absolute possession…

Memory scorched within her, sending blood rushing to her face. She looked away immediately, willing her high colour to subside, digging her nails into her palms.

'Cream with your coffee?'

Luca's deep voice penetrated her agitation, and with forcible effort she turned to him, making her face expressionless.

'Thank you,' she said.

He handed her a cup, pushing the jug towards her, and she thankfully busied herself pouring in cream, stirring as she did so, watching, as if it were a fascinating movie, how the rich cream swirled into the dark, aromatic coffee.

'Sugar?'

Luca's deep voice came again, but this time Ariana shook her head.

'Sweet enough already?'

His jibe was open, and it made her eyes flash to him. 'And I have reason to be *sweet* right now because…?' she retorted, just as jibing.

Something darkened in his slate-grey eyes and she saw a momentary tightening of his mouth.

'Perhaps because I've thrown you a financial lifeline to save your business?' He matched her retort.

She was silent, jaw set, knowing she could not answer back this time. She lifted her cup with a jerky movement, took an unwise mouthful of hot coffee. But she made no show of how hot it had been. Made no show of anything she felt.

He was speaking again, his voice silky. 'So a little more appreciation of my…generosity…would not go amiss, hmm?'

His eyes were resting on her as he sat back, crossing one long leg over the other, making himself comfortable as he held his coffee cup, stirring the cream in a leisurely fashion.

What was in that gaze except a toxic taunt…? Oh, dear God. That rush of colour threatened yet again. There was a hint of what she knew must come… Both reminiscence over that fateful, torrid night of sex in New York and anticipation of a repeat performance.

Was he expecting her to reply to what he'd just said? The words choked in her throat and she dropped her eyes to her coffee cup, busying herself with taking another sip, less scalding this time.

He let her drink uninterrupted, and as she did so she could feel the caffeine start to hit. Bringing everything into focus. She lifted her eyes to the man sitting opposite her. His own eyes were still resting on her. In the soft light she could not make out their expression. But she did not need to. She knew what would be in them.

She set down her empty coffee cup, got to her feet. His eyes followed her as she crossed the narrow space between them. He put down his own cup, got to his feet as well. Less than a metre from her. She caught the scent of his aftershave—the same as he'd worn in New York.

For a second she felt faint… Then she forced herself to speak. To say what she must say. Or lose what was most precious to her…

'You said…' Ariana heard her own voice as if it came from a long, long way away '…you wanted my…appreciation.'

He looked at her, his gaze unreadable, but she saw the tightness of his mouth, the steeling of his jaw.

'Tell me,' she went on, and she could hear the husk in her voice, knew why it was there, 'if I show you my… appreciation…what will you do for me? Will you write off the loan you hold over my head? So that I need not to repay it?'

He was standing stock-still, but he lifted a hand, reaching forward. His forefinger brushed down her cheek. Slowly, consideringly. It felt like a burning brand, searing her skin.

Branding me. Owning me. Body and soul.

He gave her his answer, his voice an open taunt, 'Perhaps that depends on just how appreciative you are.'

His long lashes dipped over his eyes, then lifted, and in their pitiless depths she could see all that she feared.

'Perhaps,' he said, and now he drew his forefinger down her throat, 'you might give me a demonstration?'

She felt his finger like the blade of a knife. As if it were drawing blood. He wanted *her* to make the move.

Wanted *her* to commit the act that he required—her abject surrender. Her complete humiliation.

But she had been humiliated by him before.

And she would never, *never* let him do so again.

Never. Whatever it costs me!

Her business could go down the drain…she could lose everything she possessed—but not what was most precious to her. The one thing she would never lose again.

My self-respect. That is all I care about now—all that is vital to me. Essential!

Defiance blazed in her. A sheet of fury, white-hot and lethal. In a sudden jerking movement she stepped away, head snapping back, hands flying up to ward him off. There was denial in every line of her body. Scorn in her flashing eyes. Words spat from her. And there was absolute refusal in them, lashing like a whip.

'In your dreams! In your *dreams*, Luca Farnese—because you'll get nothing else! *Nothing!* I'd starve in a gutter first!'

Vehemence seared her like a branding iron on flesh as she reared back from him, from what he wanted of her, what he thought he could reduce her to. Begging from him with her body.

His reaction was so fast she could not foresee it, let alone avoid it. Hands snaked out, seized her shoulders, fastening over them like iron. And what was in his face now she had never seen before.

'*Dreams?* Of *you*?' A harsh, mocking laugh broke from him, cut off with a contortion of his features. 'Do you know why I summoned you here tonight? Let you think you could prostitute yourself for me?'

The iron grip of his hands tightened, his fingers digging into her. His voice had been a snarl, and it came again now.

'So I could do exactly what I'm doing now! Throw you from me like rotten flesh!'

His hands lifted from her as though she were poison, contaminated, and the movement was so sudden she reeled back as if he had actually flung her from him.

His voice was low, feral, his eyes like dark pits of fire. 'Do you think I would *ever* sully myself on you again? A woman like *you*?'

She stumbled back, hands flailing helplessly, trying to get her balance. Her face contorted. Mouth twisting as she heard what he'd just hurled at her.

Her voice choked as she spat back at him. It was all she could do. 'Go to *hell*, Luca Farnese! Just go to *hell*!'

She lurched away, snatching up her evening bag, half stumbling to the door of the suite, long skirts twisting around her legs, impeding her. She had to get out of there…she was suffocating, drowning…

From the moment Luca Farnese had told her to her face that he would take her to his bed again she had vowed to reject him with all the scorn and fury she was capable of. And all along…

All along he'd been planning a completely different kind of humiliation. Even crueller.

A choking sound broke from her and she clutched at the door handle, trying to yank the door open, fumbling with the catch because she was shaking, desperate, beyond anything, only wanting to escape—flee, get away…

She couldn't bear to be here—couldn't bear to breathe the same air as him.

Couldn't bear it…

A hand closed over her shoulder again like an iron vice, hauling her around. 'You're going nowhere!'

He towered over her, eyes like dark fire, face twisted in rage. Rage at her defiance? Her escape? She didn't know. Didn't care. Knew only that she had to breathe fresh air—or drown.

'Let me go!' Her voice was piercing—desperate.

Her eyes flared upwards, into his. And out of nowhere fear filled her. Not fear of his physical hold on her, which was lessening even as the fear seized her. But a fear that came from a far more terrifying place…

From herself. Her own body…

Treacherous—betraying.

The grip on her shoulder changed. His mouth untwisted. Only the dark fire in his eyes remained.

Pouring into her.

Burning into her.

For one endless moment they stood, frozen in time.

Then she spoke again: 'Let me go.' It was a halting, faltering whisper. A plea.

Slowly, infinitely slowly, her gaze agonising, she watched him shake his head.

'I can't.' A rasp broke from him. 'I can't let go of you—' he said.

And yet his hand dropped from her shoulder and she felt her body sway with the release of his grip. She must turn away—walk away—she *must*…

But she did not move. The world had stopped—so

had her breathing, her pulse, the very beat of her heart. All had stopped. And still she could not move. His eyes were burning into hers, with a dark, dark fire in their bottomless depths. She could not wrench hers away. Could do nothing…

She heard him say her name. A hollow husk. Saw his hand lift to her waist. Felt weakness drown her…

His hand moved around her waist slowly, infinitely slowly, and she knew with what was left of any consciousness within her that she must step back—that stepping back, leaving, was the only sane thing to do…

But there was no sanity any longer. No sense, no consciousness…no rage or scorn or anger or fury. Only the flame beating up in her, burning all her senses, possessing her…

He said her name again, low and hoarse and broken. He stepped towards her, drawing her to him, his hand splaying out over her spine.

She was pliant, yielding…

Yielding to what was possessing her. Consuming her.

Even as her mouth, lips parting, lifted to his…

CHAPTER EIGHT

HER MOUTH WAS VELVET. Velvet and silk and honey and nectar. He could only gorge on it. Everything dissolved around him. All sense…all shame. All purpose but this.

Somewhere he heard the sound of words shredding in his head like torn rags. This was not what he'd intended…

She was supposed to have come here—supplicant, desperate—and I was to have let her come, let her believe that I would allow her to do what she thought I was offering her. And then, when the moment came and she offered herself to me, I would thrust her from me—cast her aside. Show her that she had nothing that I wanted! Show her she had no power over me. Show myself that she has no power over me...

The very thought was a searing mockery to him now. She was in his arms, her body pressed to his, her mouth opening to his. His mouth was devouring hers and hers his. Desire—urgent…desperate—was leaping in them both. Desire that was impossible to deny. To defeat…

Her breasts were cresting against him and he could feel his arousal spearing him, widening his stance, could feel her hips crushing into his, feel the blinding flame of desire flare up in her as it did in himself. Unquenchable…consuming everything. His will, his reason, his conscious mind.

All evening he had fought it—from the moment she'd walked in, so incandescently alluring, just as she had been that first fatal evening when her lush, wanton beauty had inflamed him. But he had steeled himself, exerted his iron strength to see this through to the end. To the moment when he would complete his destruction of her.

By rejecting her.

Rejecting who she was and what she had done to him. What she would never do to him again.

What she was doing now…

Blindly he lifted her into his arms, felt the ripe lushness of her body pressing against his as he carried her into his bedroom.

Into his bed.

His whole body was aflame for her. Consuming him in its fire.

Light was filtering through shuttered windows. Light that burnt.

Ariana opened her eyes.

Luca was standing there, looking down at her. He had on a bathrobe. His jaw was unshaven. Eyes like granite. For an endless moment he simply went on looking at her, nothing in his eyes, in his face. Nothing at all.

Then he turned and walked into the en suite bathroom.

Then silence.

She turned her head aside. Inside her chest her heart started to thud. The drum beats of a funeral.

Slowly, agonisingly, she made herself get out of bed. Made herself find her clothes, struggle into the evening gown that was on the floor, force her feet into her sandals. Made herself walk out of the bedroom, find her handbag, head for the door.

She was about to walk out of another hotel room, another hotel. Another city. But away from the same man. Déjà vu all over again…

Except for one small detail.

As she opened the door a voice behind her sounded. Harsh. Low. And taut as a garotte.

'I used no protection—I had none with me.'

Ariana turned, horror filling her.

It was the worst two weeks of Ariana's life.

If she had thought the days following her precipitate flight from New York unbearable, that was nothing, nothing at all, compared to each and every day now, that crawled with agonising slowness towards the due date of her next period. Only then could she be sure that any pregnancy test would be accurate and not a false negative.

Because she could not risk that! Could not risk feeling the desperate relief that the disaster of that hellish night had not resulted in what she feared most. She could not risk thinking she was safe—and then find she was not.

And when her regular-as-clockwork period failed to arrive she knew, with the same horror that had possessed her when Luca had thrown his declaration at her, that all her desperate hope had been in vain. A knowledge confirmed, like a vice crushing all the air out of her lungs, as she stared two days later at the vivid blue line on the pregnancy test stick.

Only one shred of hope was left for her to cling to. The lie she had managed somehow, with a strength she had not known she still possessed, to throw back at Luca before she'd made her escape from him.

'Don't worry—I'm protected!'

She had thrown it at him in a defiant snarl and from an impulse that had overridden everything else. Because there was only one thing worse than her being pregnant by Luca—and that was him knowing it.

Cold ran down her spine now as she took in the implications of that blue line. Pregnant. She was pregnant. She had conceived Luca's baby. She wanted to laugh—a hysterical, demented laugh. Because what other response could she give to such a realisation? Instead, she found her arms going around her midriff, in a protective gesture as old as time.

But there was only one person she must protect her baby from.

Its father.

Luca was working. He was working every hour God sent and then some. He was flying around the world. Working on the plane. Working in the hotels he stayed at. Working when he was back in his apartment in Milan, long into the early hours. Working to forget.

To blank. To block.

To deny.

Deny his own insanity.

Deny what he had done…what he had succumbed to. What he had committed.

How could I have done it? How could I?

He stared darkly and unseeing at his computer screen, the words and the numbers blurring into an incomprehensible mass.

A mess as incomprehensible as the criminal folly of what he had done.

Taken Ariana to his bed again.

The one woman in all the world he did not want to want.

Ariana was planning. Planning with an urgency that was driving her like a demon. First to work to a punishing schedule, finishing off every project, banking all the money she could—her survival fund.

It would not be much, but it would be essential. It would get her to the UK where she would try to live and work. Staying first with Mia and Matt, she'd use her contacts to get a job. See out her pregnancy, either as a designer or, at worst, a saleswoman. Her own business was finished—it had been since Luca had shown himself to be her mystery money lender.

Her own words seared in her memory.

'I'd sooner starve in a gutter!'

She gave a thin smile. Well, it would not be a gutter, and she would not quite starve, but everything would go—from the last bolt of fabric to her racy little car. Luca could pick the bones of her business clean if he so wanted. But that was all he would get.

Nothing else.

Instinctively—protectively—Ariana's splayed hand dropped again to her midriff…

Luca's mobile was ringing.

'Si?' His voice was curt as he took the call. He knew who it was, or he would not have answered.

'There is news, Signor Farnese.'

The caller's tone was neutral. Carefully so.

'And?'

Luca's expression did not change as he listened.

But something inside him changed.

His whole world changed.

Ariana gave a last glance around her bedroom. A pang smote her. She was losing what she had taken her adult life to build—an independence that was hers and hers alone. Now she must make a new life—for herself and her baby.

She hefted up her single suitcase—all she was taking with her. She gave a sour smile. Luca could make what use he wanted of her designer outfits. She would have no use for them as her pregnancy increased, nor in the penny-pinching life she must lead from now on. He could pass them on to the next woman whose life he destroyed.

But he didn't destroy Mia's life by marrying her—and he won't destroy mine.

That was all that mattered.

Face set, she walked downstairs, letting herself out

on to the street. She would post the keys to her accountant—he could hand them on to Luca Farnese.

Except that would not prove to be necessary.

Because Luca was waiting for her on the pavement.

He could see shock whiten her face, deepening the hollows under her eyes. She did not look well. Her unmade-up face was gaunt, her hair pulled back into a tight knot. And she was too thin. Surely she should be gaining weight, not losing it?

His eyes went instinctively to her waistline. She was wearing jeans and a cotton sweatshirt. He frowned. Had his information been wrong? For a piercing second emotion stabbed him—but he did not know what it was and he put it from him. She was still standing there, frozen with shock, completely motionless.

'Going somewhere?' he asked pleasantly.

He levered himself away from the bonnet of his car, drawn up half on the pavement.

'Yes.'

A single word. Stony. As stony as her face.

'But not, however,' he informed her, his voice still pleasant, 'where you thought you would be going.' He paused. Then spoke again. 'I've had you under surveillance since you walked out on me. You see, Ariana...' and now he made his voice like silk '...you have a habit of lying, and so I questioned your claim that you had been protected from pregnancy as you asserted. Your visit to a pharmacy to buy a pregnancy test might just have been caution on your part, to check you weren't pregnant—but your attending an antenatal clinic could only confirm that you were.'

Was it possible for her ashen face to whiten more? It did. He stepped towards her, taking her suitcase, tossing it into the boot of his car, then opening the passenger door.

'We need to get going, Ariana. I want to be in Milan this evening, and it's a three-and-a-half-hour drive.'

For a moment she only looked at him. The shock was lifting from her face, and something else was taking its place.

Closure. Complete closure. As if there were no longer a person behind the mask of her face.

She stepped forward, got into the passenger seat, did up her seatbelt as he took his own place behind the wheel and started the engine. He could still feel emotion running within him like an underground river, deep beneath the rock. Eating away at it from the inside.

She did not speak as he nosed the car forward. He did not care. Her response was not necessary. Her wishes did not matter.

Nor do mine.

The buried emotion jack-knifed in him like a stiletto thrust into his lungs. He thrust it back, down into his guts, where it must stay, its sharp edges like a razor embedded in his flesh. He would get used to its presence eventually. He would have to.

'Why are you doing this?'

Her abrupt question made his hands tighten over the steering wheel. He did not bother to ask what she meant by 'this'.

'The future has changed for both of us. It is necessary for us to accept the consequences of that change.'

He could see her head twisting towards him. In her lap, her hands were folded over her handbag. Only the white of her knuckles showed the tension she was under.

'It isn't a future that need concern you,' she replied.

Luca felt his jaw tighten—a sign of the self-control he was exerting. The self-control he always had to exert around her.

Except when it fails—catastrophically. And thus brings me to this point, now, where my life has been hijacked.

He wanted to laugh…a savage humourless laugh. Instead, halting at red lights, he simply glanced at her, his eyes flickering.

'Does the irony of it not strike you, Ariana? That the lie you told the world at my wedding has now become the truth?'

Her head turned away, dipped. 'Irony isn't the only word for it.'

'No,' he agreed, his voice low and tight.

The lights changed and he had to look ahead again. They were gaining the outskirts of the city. The autostrada awaited them, and then the long drive to Milan. And the even longer journey into a future that he had never wanted. That he had spent his life not wanting.

His grip on the steering wheel increased…the razor in his guts twisted.

She was speaking again, but not looking at him this time, her voice still low. Intense.

'Let me go, Luca. I will sign whatever disclaimers

you require. Make no demands on you—financial or otherwise. Make no mention of you on the birth certificate. I will sever all contact with you, have nothing more to do with you. Leave you entirely free of me. Free of—'

She got no further.

'That will not happen.' His voice was hard. 'Because what *will* happen is this. We shall marry.'

Ariana heard him say it, but she did not believe it. It was impossible to believe. Impossible because it was… *impossible*.

Her eyes flew to him. There was only his profile, aquiline, carved from granite. Unyielding.

She shut her eyes, turning her head away from him, subsiding into silence. A profound weariness swept over her. These last weeks had been punishing—working non-stop, making what preparations she could, dismantling of her old life, ready for the construction of her new one. She felt….drained.

The smoothness of the car ride started to lull her to sleep, the sun streaming in warming her. Her thoughts wandered, become random, a blur. Her breathing slowed…

Her eyes were too heavy to open again. She wanted only to shut the world away.

Escape the only way she could.

Into sleep.

Luca slotted his car into his section of the underground car park at the block of luxury apartments in which he owned the entire top floor, parking it between his low-slung supercar and the top-of-the-range SUV he drove when heading for the Lakes or the Alps. Cutting the engine, he looked at Ariana asleep beside him. In repose, even in the dim light of the car park, she looked…

Beautiful.

The word was in his head before he could stop it. His eyes rested on her. Her head was tilted back, in three-quarter profile. The shadows under her eyes seemed less deep, the perfection of the sculpted features more accentuated. Her mouth more tender.

There was something familiar about her—and yet something *un*familiar. Something that was not her as he remembered her. Something…

Like Mia.

His gaze flickered. For the first time he could see the family resemblance. Their parents, after all, had been siblings…

He shook himself mentally. Cousins the two of them might be, Mia and Ariana, but in temperament, and in character, they could not be more different. And yet it was a disturbing thing, to see the faint resemblance between them, even though one was so dark and one so fair, one so gentle and one so—

Memory flared in him. Ariana, hurling her vitriolic denunciation at him in that elevator lobby in New York, her face contorted—as contorted as it had been at the hotel in Lucca—telling him to go to hell. The memories fused. Fused with more. His mother's rages…

He thrust open his car door to banish the memories—all of them—and the sound awakened Ariana. She opened her eyes, startled.

'We're here,' he told her, getting out of the car, going around to the boot to remove her suitcase.

She got out too, following him wordlessly to the elevator. It swept them up to his penthouse apartment. Inside, he led the way from the entrance hall down a short corridor, opening up a door.

'Your bedroom,' he said.

He went in, deposited her suitcase, and Ariana followed him in, gazing about her, saying nothing still.

'Freshen up,' he said, 'then join me in the lounge.'

She didn't answer, and he left her. Emotions were roiling inside him again, and he needed to be away from her right now.

He strode into his own bedroom—the master suite. It occupied the other flank, away from the entrance hall. It seemed prudent to put as much space between them as the apartment afforded.

More than prudent.

Essential.

CHAPTER NINE

ARIANA LIFTED THE lid of her suitcase, got out her toiletries bag, then disappeared into the en suite bathroom. It was as starkly modern as the bedroom. She washed her face and hands, staring for a while at her reflection. A blank-faced woman looked back at her with nothing in her eyes. Nothing at all.

Why did I come here? Why did I get into that car... let him drive me here?

Why had she not raged, or screamed, or run, or fought…?

But she knew the answer—had known it from the moment she had set eyes on him on the pavement. With a sense of exhaustion, inevitability—defeat.

There had been no point in not going with him. Now that he knew about the baby everything had changed.

She heard again his voice, saying what was unbelievable—unthinkable. Impossible even to contemplate.

'We shall marry.'

She pushed herself away from the vanity unit. Why had he even bothered to say it? Of *course* they would not marry…

Another wave of exhaustion ran through her—not physical as such, but far deeper. For now, all she could do was what she was doing. Not thinking, not feeling… not wanting to. It was all she had the energy for.

She emerged from the bathroom, feeling fresher in face than in spirit, then left the bedroom, making her way back down the corridor and into the front hall. A huge reception room opened off it. Again, the décor was starkly modern. Punishingly expensive. She could tell that at a glance. Plate glass windows marched down the far wall, and a wide terrace was beyond, illuminated with bold lights. To the right, a dining room opened up, and beyond it she could glimpse a kitchen.

Then Luca was walking in. He had changed out of his business suit, swapping it for well-cut trousers and a cashmere sweater, and Ariana frowned. She had never, she realised, seen him in casual wear. In New York he'd been in a tux, in Lucca in a business suit. And in church, at his wedding, he'd been in a morning suit.

She hauled her mind away, not wanting to remember that hideous scene. She couldn't bear it. A wave of depression swept over her. Had there truly been no other way of saving Mia from a marriage she did not want to make, but did not dare to refuse? A way that didn't end in bringing herself here, like this? Pregnant by the man whose wedding she had ruined, who loathed her very guts for what she'd done…

'What would you like to drink?'

Luca's enquiry was polite as he crossed to a sideboard made of chrome and walnut, which Ariana had disliked on sight.

'Mineral water—still,' she replied. 'I can't take *frizzante* any longer.'

He glanced at her.

She gave a slight shrug. 'I've had some morning sickness.'

His obsidian eyes assessed her. 'Is that why you've lost so much weight?' His question sounded more of an accusation than an enquiry.

'I don't know,' she answered.

He opened a bottle of mineral water, poured it for her, and came across to where she stood in the middle of the room.

'It can't be good for you…losing weight. You should be putting it on.'

'I'm not even past my first trimester,' she said.

She took the glass from him, taking a sip. Her throat was dry, suddenly. To be here—here in Luca Farnese's ultra-modern, ultra-luxurious penthouse apartment in Milan—discussing her pregnancy, was unreal.

She felt emotion clutch at her and took another sip of water.

'I'm well aware of that,' was the only reply she got.

He'd returned to the sideboard, poured himself a shot of whisky from a bottle that she recognised as one of the most expensive single malts. He knocked it back, poured himself another, then threw himself down on a black leather sofa which Ariana had also immediately disliked. She disliked every aspect of the décor.

Yet it suits him.

The acknowledgement was in her head before she

could stop it. The stark, unyielding décor was a perfect match for this stark, unyielding man.

He sat back, one arm thrown out across the back of the sofa, one long leg angled over his thigh. An apparently relaxed attitude, but she had never seen a man less relaxed. Her eyes went to his face, and she felt her throat tighten at its impact on her. Protest against it as she would…

Why? Why this man? Why him? What is it? What does he have? Why does he do to me what he does and why do I respond to it? To him? Why do I just want to gaze and gaze at him? To drink in every feature, feel every impact of it? Why? Why am I so helpless?

The questions tumbled through her head but she could not answer them. Not a single one.

He was taking another mouthful of his whisky, then he looked at her straight on. 'Dinner will be here soon—there are kitchens in the apartment block that provide room service.'

She gave a slight nod, taking a seat on the sofa opposite him, clutching her glass of water.

He was silent for a moment. Then… 'We need to talk.'

She looked at him, saying nothing. What was there to say? Except… 'I'm not marrying you.'

The words fell from her lips and she was glad she had said them. Glad that she had made it clear. Where he had got the insane notion from she didn't know or care.

She saw his grip on his glass tighten. His jaw tightened.

His eyes lanced hers. 'Yes,' he told her, 'you will.'

She changed her expression changed, let it become one of genuine enquiry.

'Luca, why do you say that? Why do you even talk of marriage? It's so insane it doesn't bear thinking of!' She took a razoring breath. 'You cannot possibly want to marry me—'

'Of course I do not.' The words were stark. The voice harsh. 'You are the very last woman on earth I would want to marry.'

It was like a physical blow. As if he'd brought his hard, pitiless hand slashing down on her. But how could it be a blow? How could it? A blow—physical or verbal—would hurt, and how could she be hurt by what he'd said?

Not any longer. Not since that morning in Manhattan, when she'd run out of the hotel room to see him waiting by the elevator. Walking out on her after a night that had been so…so…

'But we have no choice, Ariana—neither you, nor I.'

He cut across the memories she must not have. Memories that were forbidden her, too cruel to remember.

His voice was still harsh and she could only go on looking at him, unable to turn away, to hide, to find any protection or shelter from him. Just as she had been unable to find any protection or shelter from the words he'd dropped like stones, crushing her, breaking her ribs, her lungs, as those elevator doors had opened for him.

'I'm returning to Italy to be married.'

With jerking hands she raised her glass to her lips, bone-dry again, and took another jolting sip, her eyes dropping down as if to protect herself from his rejecting gaze.

Rejecting her…not wanting her. Not wanting her for anything other than what he'd already had of her.

And not even wanting that now. Not even in his dreams.

In her head she heard his cruel, mocking words that night in Lucca, when he'd excoriated her with his rejection of her.

'Dreams? Of you? Do you think I would ever sully myself on you again?'

Her grip on her glass of water tightened to painfulness, numbing her fingertips with the pressure she was exerting. It was as if the pressure were around her throat, choking her. Choking her with the truth she had to face.

Luca Farnese—not wanting her…

Not wanting her that nightmare morning-after in Manhattan.

Not wanting her in that hideous scene in his hotel room in Lucca.

Not wanting her now, in this nightmare.

He was forcing himself to marry her—because for a second time she had committed an act of such criminal folly that she must pay for it all her life.

But my baby will not pay! I will not allow that!

Fierce emotion seared through her. Her eyes snapped up again.

'Yes—yes, we *do* have a choice! A choice I will exercise and to hell with you! I will have this baby on my own, and you will not have to force yourself to have anything to do with it—anything to do with me!'

She felt her jaw clench, her eyes burning with fire as she ploughed on, saying what had to be said—what had to be faced. By her—and by him. Her voice was ragged, but she would not let it break. By force of will she spoke vehemently, desperately…

'You've never wanted me for anything but sex! I've known that—and faced it!—ever since that morning in New York! You used me then like I was a whore—a sex toy—something to slake your passing lust with! Knowing all the time that you were going to be married to another woman—knowing it all the time you were having sex with me! And if you think…if you think that I would ever, *ever* let a man like that have *anything* to do with an innocent baby—*my* baby!—then—'

His voice cut across hers like a scalpel, eviscerating her.

'And do you think that I would ever want the mother of a child of mine to be a woman so jealous, so vindictive, that she would do what you did to your own cousin? A woman who had done you no harm—none! Who could never harm anyone! The gentlest, sweetest soul—'

A smothered cry broke from her and she turned away, gulping at her water, wishing it were whisky so that she could drown herself in its oblivion. She was shaking—shaking like a leaf—and she could not hold her glass steady. Water was splashing on to her chest, her lap…

Suddenly the glass was taken from her. Set down on the glass and chrome coffee table—another item of furniture she hated. But then hatred was all that was in her now…all that was knifing through her, hatred and fury and rage and destruction…

She felt the sofa dip beside her, felt her hands being taken. She was shaking still, but the hard, large hands folding around hers would not let them shake. Her eyes jolted upwards. Luca was seated beside her, his hands tight over hers. He was speaking—she could hear his words. But they could not be his, surely… For they were not harsh and hating…

They were weary.

'Ariana—stop. I will too. We must. Both of us.' A heavy breath was exhaled from him. 'Somehow we have to deal with this. We *have* to…'

He drew her to her feet, and she could not help but rise with him.

'Come and eat,' he said, and his voice was still weary. Dispassionate.

He let go her hands and they felt cold suddenly—which was strange, for surely they had been colder clutching the glass of water. She levered herself up, effort though it was, and followed him into the dining room. The table—more glass and chrome—was already set for two, and she sank down gratefully on the chair at its foot. Luca sat down at the head.

A moment later Ariana heard voices in the kitchen beyond, and the clink of crockery.

'There's an entrance to my kitchen from the service elevator,' Luca informed her, as two young women came into the dining room, carrying small plates.

He murmured something to them and they both smiled at him. Ariana could tell they were impressed by him, responding to his lethal looks, his air of understated wealth and power. *Poor fools,* she thought, and then envied them for not knowing his true nature.

He gave a cool nod and they set down the plates. One of them fetched a bottle of opened wine from the kitchen, presenting it to him and receiving another cool nod in return, while the other wheeled in a trolley bearing two large plates with silvered covers, and two dessert plates containing *tarte au citron.*

'Grazie,' Luca said to them, and nodded in dismissal. They disappeared silently, closing the kitchen door behind them.

Ariana looked down at the plate in front of her. Some kind of vegetable terrine with dressed leaves. She wondered if she felt hungry, but she could not tell.

'You need to eat.'

Luca's voice came from the far end of the table and mechanically she picked up her fork and made a start. It was, in fact, delicious. Maybe she was hungry after all. Her eating had been erratic these last weeks as she'd worked every hour on finishing off client projects, snatching sandwiches here and there, nothing more than that.

Luca poured himself a glass of white wine, but did not offer her any. She stuck to water.

She went on eating, steadily demolishing the terrine and then reaching for a bread roll, consuming that too. It seemed strange to be dining with Luca Farnese again—although 'strange' was an understatement if ever there was one.

The third time I've done so.

But this time would be different from the previous two. This time… She felt her throat tighten. This time she would not be falling into bed with him…

She yanked her mind from the thought. Danger lapped at her like a dark, drowning tide. She pushed her empty plate away. Luca had finished too, and without speaking he got to his feet, picking up his own plate and collecting hers, replacing them with the larger plates, removing the silver covers.

It was chicken in a lightly creamy sauce, with new potatoes and French beans. It, too, was delicious, and Ariana realised she was eating with a will. But that was all. Otherwise an air of unreality was possessing her. Right now she should be landing in London, ready to remake her life. Instead—

Her thoughts cut out. It was impossible to think of anything right now.

Impossible to accept what was happening or where she was.

Impossible.

She heard Luca start to speak, cutting across her thoughts.

'So,' he said, 'where were you heading off to?'

She forked another mouthful of tender chicken. 'I was leaving Italy,' she said tonelessly.

'America, perhaps? Your mother? You mentioned that evening in New York that she lives in Florida now.'

Ariana glanced at him. 'My mother? No! She's the last person I'd go to!' There was more expression in her voice now. 'I know exactly what she'd tell me about my being pregnant. She'd tell me to get rid of it!' Something emptied out of her voice as she went on. 'The way she's always told me she wishes she'd done with me—'

She broke off, seizing up her water and taking a gulp. Luca's eyes stayed on her. She looked across at him, meeting them square-on. If Luca Farnese wanted the whole sorry tale he could have it, and he'd be welcome to it.

'She got pregnant at nineteen by the man she'd run off with—my father. Who was a fortune-hunter. Plus a gambler and an alcoholic. She's always said he got her pregnant deliberately, in order to increase the size of the pay-off he was after from my grandfather.'

She paused, eyeballing Luca. His face was expressionless.

'It's not an edifying tale.' She gave a half-shrug of her thin shoulder. 'Well, he got his pay-off and I got his name—he had to marry my mother as part of the deal my grandfather insisted on. Then he got a speedy divorce the moment I arrived in the world. My mother went back to my grandfather, but bolted again the moment she could—yet another elopement. This time, luckily for her, with a man who could afford her. As for me… I was left at the *palazzo*.'

Her expression changed. Softened without her realising it.

'My uncle and his wife took me on. They lived there. My uncle was a gentle soul, and so was his wife—it's where Mia gets her sweet nature from, I suppose—and, unlike my mother, my uncle never defied his father.' She paused, and her eyes suddenly had a faraway look, as if she was back in a past long-vanished. 'I was happy with them… Even after Mia was born they were still kind and affectionate towards me. It might all have worked out OK, except—'

She broke off again.

'Except?' There was a new note in Luca's voice.

Ariana only gave that half-shrug again.

'My aunt and uncle were killed in a car crash when I was eight and Mia five. After that—' She swallowed and then went on, resignation in her voice. 'I reacted badly—I became "wilful and difficult", as my grandfather calls it. I was packed off to my mother, who was on her third husband by then, and living in Paris. She had absolutely no wish for me to be there, no interest in me. I was a nuisance to her and her latest husband, so I was returned to the *palazzo*—where my behaviour got even worse. I was sent away to school. A convent, where I was a boarder. I came home for Christmas, that was all, when I was allowed to see Mia—allowed to see that she had become my grandfather's most adored granddaughter. So pretty, so gentle, so pleasing in her manners…like a little doll.'

'And you resented her for that.' There was a harshness in Luca's voice.

Ariana did not answer. Resentment was the last thing she'd felt. She'd felt only a heart-wrenching, pitiful envy of Mia, so loved by her grandfather. Whereas she herself…

Unwanted—rejected. By my father, my mother, my grandfather. None of them ever wanted me. Cared anything about me.

She stopped remembering. There was no point to it.

No point in explaining to Luca or even trying to. She knew what he thought of her. He would not change that… whatever pitiful tale she might trot out to him.

So she just gave another shrug. Went on eating…

'So…' Luca's voice came again '…if you weren't going to your mother, where were you going?'

'Ireland,' Ariana lied.

She didn't want him knowing about her plan to live in London. Didn't want him to know anything about Mia—that she had married another man, preferring Matt to him.

If he knew the truth about why I stopped the wedding—because his bride was desperate for a way to avoid marrying him—would he seek to punish her as he has punished me?

It was a chilling thought—and she knew she must do all she could to protect her gentle, fearful cousin. Luca Farnese could crush her and Matt like eggshells…

'To the Irish side of your family?' he probed.

'No,' she said shortly. 'I know nothing about them.'

He frowned. 'Your father…?'

'I have no idea about him—he could be dead for all I know. Like I say, he was an alcoholic. I don't know of any relatives, and even if I did I wouldn't want to know them.'

'So why go to Ireland?'

She shrugged again. 'It's somewhere to go.'

She saw him reach for his wine, a frown still on his face. 'Why leave Italy? Your work is based here.'

'Was,' she corrected. She set down her knife and fork.

Looked straight at him. 'I won't be repaying your loan. So the bank will foreclose on me.'

'Obviously that won't apply now!' His voice was sharp. Then he set down his wine glass. Looked straight at her. 'Things have changed between us, Ariana. That much is obvious. I won't object to your continuing to work in moderation—for a while, at least. Afterwards, when the baby is born… Well, we shall see. Working mothers are not, after all, uncommon.'

She picked up her cutlery again, resumed eating.

'I'm not marrying you, Luca, and whether I am a working mother or not will be none of your concern. I won't be living in Italy, and I won't be asking for, let alone accepting, any child maintenance. You won't be involved in any way.'

She did not let emotion enter her voice. There was no reason for it to do so. She was simply stating what was going to happen.

His voice cut across her grim, bleak thoughts.

'Do you want me to contest custody?'

CHAPTER TEN

IT WAS CALMLY SAID. Dispassionately said.

Ariana's cutlery clattered to the plate.

'On what grounds?'

Now there was emotion in her voice.

'On the grounds that I do not want my child raised in a foreign country. Taken from me.'

His eyes were levelled on her and they were not dispassionate. They were the very opposite.

'I will fight you with everything I have to prevent that.' He paused. 'And I have a great deal to fight you with, and good reason to do so. Do you doubt it, Ariana?'

She felt every muscle in her body clench, emotion biting in her throat. Then it died away, defeated. In any custody battle Luca Farnese would win. He would use his money, his power, to hire the best lawyers, drag out the process, contest any awarding of custody to her… It would go on and on for years…

I can't face that—I just can't...

That sense of weary, bone-tired exhaustion that had made her climb into his car that afternoon now assailed her again. Defeat dragged at her…

He was speaking again, and his voice was different. 'Ariana, do you really want that? Do not try and fight me on this. You will not win.' He paused again. 'And there is no need to fight me. We can do this civilly. There does not need to be any drama.'

There was something in his voice—something that made her look at him again. His face had no expression in it, nor his eyes, but there had been a tightness in his voice.

She dropped her eyes, picked up her knife and fork, resumed eating. Then she spoke. 'We don't need to marry, Luca.'

'Ariana.' His voice cut across hers. 'Understand this from the start. I do not tolerate chaos.'

She looked at him. Whatever it was that had been in his voice a moment ago was there again.

'If we married,' she said slowly, not taking her eyes from him, 'what then?'

She did not want to know for her own sake, but simply what it was that he thought might be possible—though it would not be, for she would not be marrying him anyway…

'We legitimise our baby, establish its rights in the world, regularise its existence, secure its future.'

'And us? What happens to us?'

Again, how did he see their future? A future that was not going to happen…

He did not answer at first. Then… 'We divorce.' His eyes rested on her like weights. 'I will not chain you to me, Ariana. And…' there was the minutest pause '…and you will not chain me to you.'

He reached for his wine and drained the glass, then looked at her again. His face was expressionless, as if carved from granite.

'We are toxic for each other. Destructive.' He paused again. 'And that is why,' he told her, 'I do not want you in my life.'

His eyes rested on her. Unreadable. Implacable.

Rejecting everything about her.

Except the baby I carry—the only thing he wants of me.

There seemed to be a stone in her throat, and she looked away. But he was speaking again, and she made herself look at him, eyes blinking suddenly.

'If we accept that it will be easier,' he said. 'There will no longer be any need for…for hostility between us.'

That stone was still lodged in her throat and she could not move it, could not swallow it. She pushed her plate away, reached for her water—as if water could dissolve the stone.

Once more she saw Luca get to his feet, clear their plates away and place their dessert on the table. Mechanically she started to eat it. It was something to do.

Luca was speaking again. His voice was calm, dispassionate. Remote.

'It will not be so bad, Ariana, you know. You will get used to living here. The time will pass. As I say, you can resume your work, if you want—providing you do not exhaust yourself. My schedule is busy, as you will appreciate.' He looked at her. 'We can make this work because we must. We have no option but to do so. Both of us.'

She met his eyes. She knew there was defeat in hers. Yet it was not victory in his.

What was in them she did not know.

Nor care.

A profound weariness of spirit possessed her. For now, that was all she could face. All she could cope with.

For now…

Luca lay in his bed, motionless but not asleep. The night was passing, but sleep did not come.

He was not surprised. Only resigned.

Consciousness consumed him. Consciousness that on the other side of the entrance hall, in the guest suite, was the woman he would have given more than was rational to give not to want. Not to desire.

But desire was irrelevant now. And so were her objections to what he had told her must happen. What either of them wanted was irrelevant.

He stared up at the ceiling, trying to work out what it was he was feeling. Then realised it was nothing. And that was the best thing to feel. The only sane thing to feel. The only thing he would permit.

Memory came to him, unwanted and unbidden, but in his head for all that. Memory from so long ago. Of lying in bed, not more than ten years old, staring at the ceiling as silence had finally fallen outside his bedroom door, the shouting and the yelling over—for that night, at least. Lying there, unblinking, hands clenched at his sides, willing himself not to feel…not to feel anything at all.

It was time to feel that way again.

* * *

Ariana gazed up at the front of the Duomo, its extraordinary triangular shape intricately carved into a myriad of convoluted tracery and statuettes, a miracle of Gothic art. She turned away, making for the city's other most notable construction, the Galleria Vittorio Emanuele.

She sat herself down at a café, ordered a decaf. She missed the caffeine hit of real coffee which had so often got her through a busy working day. But her busy working days were over now.

She slumped back in her chair, sipping the unappetising coffee. Feeling quite blank. Aimless. She would fill the hours wandering around Milan. It got her out of the bleak, stark apartment that Luca called home and that suited him so well.

She'd seen him briefly when she'd surfaced, leaving for his office. He'd informed her in neutral, inexpressive tones that he was taking her to see an obstetrician the following day and had booked her in for antenatal care. She hadn't bothered to reply, and he'd left the apartment. Soon after, she'd headed out herself.

The rest of the day passed as aimlessly as she had supposed it would. She walked a lot, glad of her padded jacket as she went up and down the streets, stopping for a sandwich which she ended up feeding to the pigeons. Eventually a weariness not just of spirit but of body drove her back to Luca's apartment. She went to her bedroom, lay down on the bed, stared up at the ceiling.

Luca found her there, gazing blankly. She turned her head to look at him. He'd paused in the doorway. Her expression did not change. Her eyes were not registering his presence.

'Are you all right?'

His voice was edged. Could there possibly be concern in it? It seemed unlikely.

'Fine,' she said, and turned her head away again, staring up at the ceiling once more.

'Ariana—you can't just lie there.'

'Why not?' She did not bother to turn her head this time.

'What did you do today?'

'I walked around. It passed the time.'

She heard him cross the grey-carpeted floor, felt the mattress sink under his weight, felt her hand taken. She tried to draw it back, an instinctive gesture, but his grip tightened. Imprisoning her.

'Ariana…' his voice sounded weary now '…you have to accept what has to happen. We both do. I don't want to marry either—I don't want anything to do with you nor do you with me. We know that. Everything between us has been a mistake and should never have happened. But it did. And now…'

She heard him take a breath—a heavy one.

'Now we just have to manage the consequences. What we want is irrelevant—only the baby matters. And we have to deal with that. Somehow.'

He let go her hand and it fell back onto the bedclothes like a dead weight. She felt him stand up, heard him walk to the door again. Walk out.

She did not turn her head or move. Only as her eyes stared up sightlessly in the darkening room slow tears started. Silent and scalding, and quite, quite pointless.

* * *

Luca opened the passenger door of his car.

'Ariana…' he prompted.

Silently, she complied, getting into the low-slung car. Just as she silently complied with everything—from going to the obstetrician to coming to the table for meals. Or, as now, getting into his car.

Ariana never contested anything he told her to do.

A rapier of emotion slit him as he slid into the driver's seat. It was like the ghost of the life he'd once thought would be his. Making a marriage where there would be no drama, no discord, no angry contestation or denunciation. A marriage of only co-operation, complaisance. Agreement. A quiet, tranquil marriage. With a wife who would never subject him to the histrionics he'd grown up with, as his father had endlessly tried to placate his always angry mother.

Why had he done that? Why had his father never stood up to her?

But he knew why. Had known since he'd reached his teenage years and discovered for himself the power of female allure. His father had been in sexual thrall to his wife—a woman he could not live with or without.

Luca felt his jaw tighten, his body tense.

That's what I feared for myself—why my dreams were always of a woman like Mia.

Yet it was not Mia he was now going to marry.

He gunned the car's powerful engine, exiting the garage, making his way slowly through the Milan traffic. The weather had brightened and he was glad. He needed the elements on his side.

'Where are we going?' Ariana's question was indifferent, uninterested, and she did not look at him as she asked it.

'Somewhere that might suit you better than here,' was all the reply he made.

She made no answer to it, only went on sitting there, her hands in her lap, gazing out of the window straight ahead of her. She didn't speak again. Stayed silent.

He gained the autostrada, heading north towards their destination. Lake Como. He drove steadily, enjoying the feel of the powerful vehicle under his control. His face set. There was not much else in his life to enjoy. Had his life gone to plan he would have had Mia at his side right now. It was for Mia he'd bought the lakeside villa on Como he was now heading for—a weekend retreat from Milan for them both.

Now it was for a different woman.

The woman replacing Mia.

Displacing her.

His eyes went to the woman at his side, pregnant with his child. So utterly unlike Mia. Yet now she was as quiet as Mia, uncontesting, docilely complying with everything he said.

He felt that rapier of emotion pierce him again, engendering a chill. The words of an old warning shaped in his head.

Be careful what you wish for.

Ariana looked about her. For the first time in unnumbered days—days that had passed one after another, each as dead as the previous day, days when she had felt nothing, because nothing was all it was safe to feel and all she had the energy to feel, days of just lying on her bed for hours—it was as if something were drawing her. She felt something stir within her—a gleam of interest.

Part of her wanted to ignore it, to let it sink down into the oblivion into which she, too, wanted to sink. But without her wanting them to her eyes went to the house Luca had drawn up at, a short drive from the snaking lakeside road, secluded and private on a small promontory over the lake.

Out of long professional habit, she categorised it as her eyes rested on it. A lakeside villa, late nineteenth-century, a picturesque summer retreat from Milan. Her gaze narrowed critically. Its condition was not pristine. The exterior paint had faded and flaked and there were uneven roof tiles, a sagging porch. The gardens were bathed in autumnal sunshine. And beyond, she could see the dark indigo of the lake, silvering to obsidian.

Luca was getting out of the car and she did likewise, hardly noticing that she was doing so.

'What is this place?' she asked, looking around her.

It didn't seem like a place that he would have anything to do with. Its ornate, fin-de-siècle style could not have been more different from that stark, bleak, modernistic apartment of his in Milan.

'I bought it for Mia. A place to come at weekends… away from the city. I thought she might like somewhere like this.'

Ariana looked at him. 'Mia doesn't like water,' she said. 'She can't swim and doesn't like the sea. And she doesn't like glacial lakes. They scare her.'

She didn't wait for his response—because what could he have said other than that he had not troubled himself to ask her cousin what she might or might not like? But as she wandered off, wanting to see the villa from the front, she felt a shaft of sadness pick at her. How sad that Luca had wanted to please the woman he'd intended to marry and yet had had no idea that she would hate it…

Not that Mia would ever have told him.

And that was sad too…

She rounded the side of the villa, seeing the gardens that ran down to the water's edge, terminating in a broken paved terrace and a crumbling stone balustrade. She went to stand there, gazing out over the lake. The still, dark water was, indeed, something to fear, plunging down to icy depths so far below. But she did not share her cousin's fear of it.

She turned to survey the front of the villa, automatically itemising the work that would need doing. Inside it was probably also in need of work. She wondered what it looked like…

Luca was walking towards her. 'Shall we go inside?'

She gave a slight nod and he led the way, opening up the house for her. Inside, a flight of stairs ascended from a marble-floored hall. Some of the steps were chipped, and the walls were papered in a dated style that continued into the reception rooms, where its impact was worsened by an ugly patterned carpet and curtains. The furniture, by contrast, was antique, of the same period as the house, and it suited the ornate rooms.

Ignoring Luca, who seemed to be leaving her to it, she made her way over the whole house. Other than the dated style there was not a great deal to do, providing the plumbing and electrics were sound. Already in her head she was seeing it as *she* would do it. As if it was a commission.

When she finally re-emerged Luca was on the paved semi-circular upper terrace, and the setting sun was gilding the dark waters of the lake at the end of the garden.

'What do you make of it?' he asked.

She looked at him, then back at the neglected, run-down villa. 'It could be beautiful,' she said.

Was that wistfulness in her voice? She didn't know. Her eyes went back to Luca. He nodded. Maybe something in his austere face lightened—she wasn't sure. Or perhaps it was just the reflection of the setting sun.

'So, will you make it so?'

She started. 'Me?'

'It's why I brought you here,' he said. 'Ariana, you need a project. You're not used to being idle. You hate Milan, and my apartment. I thought this place might suit you better. That you might be less…less unhappy here.'

She swallowed, her throat suddenly tight. To have Luca Farnese show any sign of consideration for her…

But he was speaking still. 'I've talked to the obstetrician I took you to. He said…' He stopped and she saw his face tense. 'He said that you were showing signs of sinking into what might become depression. That would not be good for the baby.'

A stiletto slid into her lungs, puncturing them instantly.

It's not for me—it's just for the baby. That's all.

She swallowed again, as if she needed air.

Luca was speaking again, his words confirming that his concern was only for their baby, not herself.

'When we're married, and when the baby arrives, it will be the start of summer. This would surely be a good place to be then…fresh, clean air, away from the city…'

She made no answer. It was too much for her to deal with right now. She would not be marrying him, and she would not be living here, but there was no purpose in stating that now. She had no energy for it, no will…

For now, all I can cope with is doing what he wants – not fighting him, or contesting him, or defying him.

'So, will you take it on? Do up the villa?'

Luca's voice penetrated her wearying ever-circling thoughts and she heard herself speak—heard the familiar professional note enter her voice. It gave her something to cling to in what had become the alien landscape of her life.

'I can do an initial assessment for you…draw up some costings, provide some options,' she replied slowly. She wondered why she was offering, and then let it go. It would pass the time if nothing else.

Pass the time till when? Till you leave here and go to England, or anywhere at all? Till Luca accepts you won't marry him? Till the baby arrives...?

She heard the questions in her head but veered away from them. She didn't know and didn't have the answers.

'Good. Do so,' he replied, his tone brisk and businesslike. He got to his feet. 'Shall we go? It's getting dark and chilly. I've booked us into a hotel a short drive away.'

Ariana tensed.

Luca looked at her. 'Separate rooms,' he said drily.

His expression changed. 'It's good that you've agreed to take on this villa. I'm glad it's come in useful after all.'

Was there an edge in his voice? She didn't know and didn't care. Nor did she reply. There wasn't anything to say. As she had told him, Mia would have hated the place, and feared the water so close by. But she would have never told him so.

Poor Mia—poor, meek, biddable Mia. Pleasing everyone but herself. Letting herself be placed like a doll, never exerting any will of her own.

And now she herself was not exerting any will of her own either. She had let Luca take her over.

Have I been turning into Mia? Opting out of any agency over my own life? Letting Luca put me in his car, his apartment, while I turn my face to the wall, dissociate myself from the world, give in to his will...

She turned, looking at the villa, its faded beauty. It was unloved—sad and forlorn.

It needs a new start, a new purpose.

'Ariana?'

Luca was standing by the car, holding open the passenger door, clearly waiting for her to get in. She gave one last look at the villa, silhouetted against the darkening sky. Then got into the car.

She realised, with a strange sense of acceptance, that her mind was already running down a mental list of what the villa's refurbishment would require. That a sense of purpose was filling her…

CHAPTER ELEVEN

LUCA SAT BACK in his dining chair. They were eating at the hotel overlooking the lake, dark now except for the lights on a further shore. For the first time since the call had come through from the investigator keeping Ariana under surveillance he felt the tension racking him begin, fractionally, to ease its iron grip.

Ariana was talking, and all he had to do was sit back and listen, answering questions as and when required. She was talking about the villa, and had sketched out on hotel notepaper a new downstairs and upstairs layout. It was the first time he had seen any animation in her face since he had intercepted her planned disappearance and driven her to Milan instead, to begin the future that faced both of them.

Whether we want that future or not...

There was no choice about it. Not for him. Or for her. He had accepted it—she must too. His eyes rested on her now, his mouth tightening without his realising it. And she must not sink into the depression winding its dark tentacles around her, dulling her will to do anything other than lie on her bed, staring at the ceiling, hour after hour, going through the motions, nothing more, taking no care of herself or anything else… Passive and inert.

Docile.

The word plucked at him again, and he pushed it aside. The obstetrician's advice had been to do what he was now doing. Change the scenery and give her something to do—a project to provide her with some purpose other than simply waiting for the baby to be born. The obstetrician knew nothing of the dark conception of the baby, only that it was unplanned, unforeseen.

Into his head, disturbingly, came the memory of Ariana saying that her own mother had wished her never to have been born and her father had disowned her. She'd lost her surrogate parents, had found the loss difficult to cope with, had been sent away.

An unhappy childhood.

Like mine was.

His thoughts sheered away. He did not want to feel any similarities between them. Any kinship.

His eyes rested on her again. The new animation in her face was renewing her familiar beauty too. She had regained some weight and her face was less gaunt, cheekbones less sharp, complexion less wan. She was still not showing her pregnancy yet, but it was early days. Her first scan was still weeks away.

His thoughts sheered away again. A scan would make the baby real in a way that mere pregnancy tests and obstetric checks did not.

How can we do this? How can we bring a child into the world with parents between whom is such enmity, such discord—such anger?

But he knew the answer to that too. Had grown up with it.

Emotion stabbed in him. For that reason of all reasons he knew he must seek a better future for this child his own intemperate, disastrous weakness had created.

And that was what he was striving to do now. However appallingly Ariana had behaved—wrecking her cousin's wedding as she had, just to spite him—he had to move on from it.

And she has to move on from my leaving her. As I did after our night together in New York—a night that could never have led to anything more.

But he must not think about that night or remember it. Let alone the night that had followed.

I was supposed to break her power over me—show myself that I was not in thrall to her allure, could resist the temptation she offers. That I could defy it—deny it.

Instead…

Yet again, he steered his mind away. It was too dangerous to remember. Too dangerous to do anything but pay attention to what she was telling him now, about the possibilities presented by the villa he had bought for the bride he no longer had.

Would Mia really not have liked it? Been afraid of being so close to the lake? Surely she would have told me if that were so—why should she not have?

He shook the question away, not wanting to think about it…about a future that was gone for ever now. Facing, instead, the future that did await him.

'If you want just a light touch,' this woman he was going to have to marry instead of her cousin was saying now, 'you can leave the layout as it is, but if you want something more radical then the bedrooms can be enlarged by knocking through, and the kitchen could become a kitchen diner.'

He shook his head. 'My preference is to leave well alone as much as possible.'

Ariana nodded. 'I'm glad…' She made a start on her food—grilled fish with polenta—while Luca cut into his lamb fillet. 'A house so untouched—well, apart from the refurb thirty years ago—is rare. The kitchen will need substantial updating, as will the bathrooms, but other than the external repairs the rest of the work is nearly all cosmetic.'

'How long do you estimate it will take?'

'Given the time of year, the exterior work needs to start as soon as you give the go-ahead.'

'Do so.' He nodded.

'I've a rough idea of costs, but obviously I will get written quotes for you to approve.'

He shook his head. 'Not necessary. The cost is immaterial.'

Ariana looked across at him. 'You'll get written quotes,' she said. 'Down to the last tin of paint.'

Her gaze moved away for a moment, and he could see her thin shoulders tense.

'I'd feel safer that way…with you signing off on all the work.'

He looked at her without comprehension.

'It will protect me from you,' she said.

'Protect?'

'I can't cope with any more anger from you,' she said. Her voice was low and strained.

He was silent. Her words echoing in his head. Then… 'I don't want to be angry with you,' he said slowly.

She made no answer, only went on with her dinner.

He shook the moment from him. Yet her words lingered.

But I have cause to be angry with her. So much cause.

For ruining his hopes of marriage to Mia.

For even more than that.

For desiring her when I do not want to desire her.

His eyes went to her. She was still making absolutely no attempt to accentuate her looks. She wore no make-up, her hair was tied back, her clothes were just a sweater and a pair of casual trousers. Yet still she turned heads. There was a sensuality to her, an allure she could not conceal. He'd seen it as they'd walked into the restaurant…male eyes going to her. It was effortless for her. She seemed totally unaware of it.

He heard again the word she'd used—the one that he'd echoed.

Protect.

His mouth thinned. He was the one needing protection. From his own self, his own intolerable weakness.

From the desire for her that destroyed the life I wanted to have... Leaving me with only this.

A woman he didn't want to want.

A child that should never have been conceived.

A future it was impossible to think of but which waited for him, all the same.

* * *

Luca returned to Milan the next day and Ariana was glad.

I will always be glad when he's gone. Glad when I'm free of him.

She swallowed. Of course she would be glad. How could she not be happy to be free of a man who caused her so much torment?

For a moment—a fleeting, flying moment—she felt pain stab.

It could have been so different.

She gave a violent shake of her head. How? How could it have been different? Only if Luca had been a different man...only if he'd never wanted to marry Mia.

If he'd wanted me, not her.

But it was sweet, gentle Mia that Luca had wanted.

Into her head came the words he'd said to her that first night in Milan.

'You're the very last woman on earth I'd want to marry.'

She felt the stab of pain come again—pain that had no logic to it. Not when it was *she* who was refusing to marry *him.*

She dragged her thoughts away. Pointless to think such things, feel such things. She turned her mind, with a sense of weary relief, to what Luca had provided for her distraction.

From her base at the Lake Como hotel she started making appointments for assorted tradespersons to turn up the villa. She hired a car—a sensible run-around—to meet them there, booking them in to make an immediate start. It was familiar work, and she stepped into it easily.

Back at the hotel she emailed Luca with an initial schedule of costs, and choices for kitchen and bathroom styles, receiving by return his go-ahead and preferences.

Thoughts flittered through her consciousness. Discussing costs, finance, business, was never difficult with him. It was common ground between them… Neutral ground.

Maybe that's what we need—something that is innocuous, harmless. Nothing to do with our bitter, toxic relationship.

Did Luca feel the same way? He seemed to, and she was glad of it when he arrived for the weekend and they went over to the villa to see what had been started.

His manner was low-key as he gave her his decisions on everything from colours to kitchen units. And unlike most of her clients he made his decisions instantly.

She heard herself say as much as he drove them both back to the hotel for dinner. 'So many of my clients can't make their minds up!' she remarked. 'The worst ever is my own mother—but then, why should that surprise me? Given she can't make her mind up about her husbands, let alone her décor.'

She spoke lightly, but saw Luca glance at her as he drove.

'She seems to have made up her mind about not raising you herself. But then perhaps you were better off without her. Better no mother than one who doesn't care about you.'

There was real tension in him now. She could hear

it, and did not know why. She drew an intake of breath. What had happened to neutrality? This was raw—going deep.

And not just for me—there was something in his voice then...

She heard his words echo...about mothers who didn't care. Her eyes flickered to him, saw his profile silhouetted.

What do I know about him other than the power he has over me to make me want him? And the fact that he does not want me in return?

She felt her throat tighten. Heard herself speak. 'Well, I got used to it. Got used to being not wanted—neither by my parents nor my grandfather. Which is why...' she forced the words from her '...not being wanted by you is just par for the course really.'

It seemed important somehow for her to say that.

Perhaps it will make it easier to deal with.

She kept her head turned towards him. Only the lights from oncoming cars illuminated his stark features. It was easier to say things in the dark. Things that were difficult to say yet which needed to be said. Things she was ready to say now. Ready to face. To accept—however painful.

'I have to accept, Luca, that you don't want me,' she heard herself say. 'That you hate it that we fell into bed—twice—and that you hate me for stopping you marrying Mia. You hate, above all, that I am now pregnant. I am the very last woman, just as you told me, you'd want a baby with.' She looked away, meshing her fingers in her lap so tightly the blood flow was cut off. 'We can't help who we want or don't want in our lives.'

He did not answer and she did not expect him to. She turned her head away to look out over the dark, deadly waters of the glacial lake only a few metres from the road. Heaviness filled her, like a weight dragging her down into those deep, drowning waters, never to emerge again.

She felt tears prick in her eyes, but she could not brush them away or Luca would know that she was crying. Her throat constricted, tightening unbearably as she stifled the rising sob.

'Ariana…?

She heard him say her name. His voice low. There might have been concern in it, but that was not likely. Well, not concern for her, at any rate. For the baby, yes, but never for her.

Never.

Luca Farnese would never be concerned about her. Would never stop resenting her presence in his life. Would never want her. Would never care about her.

She had known it since that hideous morning in New York, as he'd rejected her to go back to Italy and marry the woman he *did* want—her own cousin Mia. Who did not want him. Who'd turned to *her* to save her.

And save her I did—and thus earned the enmity of this man who never wanted to want me, even for passing sex. The man whose child I now carry.

She shut her eyes, feeling that heaviness press down upon her, suffocating her. The mess of her life…the mess of his. Her thoughts burned with it. Her eyes burned with it.

It was a mess—nothing but a doomed, unholy, blighted and accursed mess...

Slow tears oozed again, scalding on her cheeks.

Then, 'Ariana—don't. Don't cry.'

Luca's voice was low, and what was in it was something she had never heard before.

In the darkness of the car's interior she felt him reach out his hand, close it over hers, still twisting in her lap. Stilling them.

'Don't cry,' he said again, and his palm was warm as it covered her hands.

A single teardrop fell, splashing his fingers and hers.

He lifted his hand away, returned it to the steering wheel. Drove on in silence.

Yet it seemed a different silence, somehow.

Luca stared down at the whisky in the glass in his hand as he stood by the window of his hotel room looking out over Lake Como, its surface dark except for where the lights of the nearby houses fell on it in shimmering pools, each separate from the other. Through the narrow wall of his room was Ariana's. Separate from his.

His thoughts were strange. Difficult.

He had strived to break her power over him—the power of his own unwanted desire for her—and he had failed. Now she was beyond him anyway—her pregnancy assured her of that.

In his head, the words she had spoken in the car circled.

'I have to accept that you don't want me.'

He wanted to laugh—savagely—at the irony of what she had said. And that was not all she had said.

'We can't help who we want or don't want in our lives.'

He heard them afresh and lifted his glass, taking a mouthful of the fiery liquid within as if it might scour out what was inside him. Deliberately, he tried to conjure an image of Mia—but it would not come. It was as if she were already a ghost in his life—faded from reality.

He lifted his eyes, stared out over the dark and deadly waters of the lake. Faced the truth he could not deny. Whoever Ariana was, whatever she did, he would always desire her.

But what else was true beyond desire?

For a moment he recalled reaching out to press her hand, feeling a tear splash on his. Tears? From this woman who had so heartlessly destroyed her cousin's wedding? Why should he have felt what he had at that moment? A kind of pity…a weary sympathy for her as she had let tears fall?

He didn't know. Couldn't know.

He could know only that his future was mapped out for him just as he had mapped hers out for her. For the sake of this child that neither of them had sought to create they must somehow—somehow…

Be better parents than those we were given.

That was the truth of it. The only truth he could allow to matter.

With a sudden movement he downed the rest of his whisky, turning away from the window. Not wanting to think about any other truths… Truths too difficult to face. Too impossible to allow.

Ariana was talking. She was saying something about the villa's electrics and taking another pastry from the basket on the breakfast table. She needed to show Luca that whatever had happened on the drive back from the villa yesterday evening, whatever show of weakness or vulnerability or unhappiness—and, most of all, that strange, haunting moment when he'd taken her hand as her tears had started to fall—she was now back on the neutral subject of its refurbishment.

He heard her out, and asked several relevant questions, but when she had answered him he took control of the conversation.

'Ariana…'

She stilled. Tensing immediately. She could tell from his tone of voice, by the pause after her name, that she needed to be tense. She closed her face, veiling her eyes. Guarding herself from him. Protecting herself.

What was he going to say? What would he hurt her with now? Surely here, in the sunlit breakfast room of this expensive hotel on Lake Como, surrounded by other guests, he could not be too hostile?

His expression had changed.

'Don't,' he said. His voice was low suddenly. 'Don't, Ariana. There is no need.'

She looked at him, her fingers tightening on the knife she was about to cut her pastry with.

'No need to look like that,' he said. 'I only wanted

to say—' He stopped. Then, 'In the car, you cried. I… I don't want you to cry.'

She swallowed, making words come, an acknowledgement come. 'Yes. I know. It's not good…' She swallowed again, more difficult this time. 'Not good for me to upset the baby.'

Something flashed in his eyes. 'It's not good for *you*,' he said. He took a breath. 'Ariana, I brought you here to the lake, to the villa, so you could do it up. In order to make things…to make things easier for you.'

He looked away, then back at her. Her expression hadn't changed and her face was still closed, she knew, her eyes veiled. Because they had to be. Not because he was going to say something hostile to her, something harsh. But because there was something in his voice, in his eyes, that she could not bear…that hurt too much.

And yet he was not wounding her with his words… So why was her throat tightening, treacherous tears prickling again in the backs of her veiled eyes?

He was speaking again, in that same low, resolute voice, with that same watchful, intent gaze on her. 'And I want things to be easier for *us*. Because there *is* an us, Ariana! Whether we ever thought there would be or not, there is now. And I just want… I want…'

He fell silent, and she could not answer him or say anything. Then he was speaking again, in that same low tone, with that same holding of her eyes. Her vision was starting to blur, so fatally…

'Last night—in my room—I… I faced a truth. About us both.'

She felt her heart stop. Her breath stop. But she did not know why.

'We neither of us had parents who put us first as children…' his voice was sombre '…and that's why *we* must for this child we have created between us. It deserves no less.'

Ariana's heart started to beat again, her lungs to fill. Whatever it was that she had thought he might say, this was no reason for not breathing, for her heart to stop.

'Maybe for each of us,' he said slowly, his gaze turning inward now, 'our childhoods help to…to explain the adults we've become.' He paused, his gaze intent. 'You grew up without parents who cared about you, jealous of your cousin, wanting what she had. Not just your grandfather's affection…you were also driven to want—'

He broke off, but Ariana knew what he had been about to say.

To want the man she had. The man who wanted her, but not you.

She felt it burn in her throat, the bitterness of it all, but he was speaking again.

'As for me—' He broke off once more. Reached for his coffee, swallowed it. Set the cup down again. Looked back at her. He was different again.

'We have to go forward, Ariana, and deal with the reality of what has happened to us. We will never be close but we can be…civilised.'

He took a breath, his expression changing. Without realising his intent, she watched as he reached his hand forward, closing it over hers as it lay inert on the tablecloth, knife handle still in its grip. He patted it, as if reassuringly, then drew back, glanced at his watch.

He got to his feet. 'And now I must be on my way,' he said, in a brisk, upbeat tone. 'I have a meeting I can't miss. I leave the villa in your capable hands—keep me updated.' He raised a hand in farewell—a casual gesture. 'Until next weekend…'

He turned, striding from the breakfast room, and was gone without even looking back.

At the table, Ariana closed her eyes. They were shimmering with diamond dewdrops. Tears there was no point in shedding. No point at all.

Luca set down his phone. His expression was taut. The necessary arrangements were all made, the paperwork complete. Now all he needed was Ariana herself. He would be fetching her from Como that morning, and by the afternoon the deed would be done.

The deed that had to be done.

For a long moment he simply stared out of his office window, wondering what it was he felt. Realising he still felt nothing. The thing it was the safest to feel. Still the safest…

The words he had said to Ariana over a month ago circled in his head.

'We can be civilised.'

Because what else was possible between them?

And what was more civilised between two people who should never have had anything to do with each than doing what had to be done for a baby that should never have existed?

And what we feel or want does not matter. Cannot matter. Can never matter.

He got to his feet, strode through into the outer office and gave his PA his instructions for the rest of the day.

He was not thinking, not letting himself think, about what the rest of the day would bring.

CHAPTER TWELVE

ARIANA WAS SHOWING Luca the newly installed kitchen.

'A distinct improvement,' was his dry judgement, before she went on to show him the rest of the villa. Its refurbishment was almost complete, done in record time—weeks instead of months. She had worked assiduously, chivvying the workmen, taking up paints and paintbrush herself in some of the rooms, because it kept her busy, kept her going, kept her from thinking or feeling.

Outwardly she was brisk, businesslike. Dealing with things on a day-by-day basis. Nothing more than that. Keeping everything else at bay.

Keeping Luca at bay.

They seemed to have settled into some kind of truce, for want of a better word. They were civil to each other—civilised, indeed, just as he had said they should be—as if all the dark, dark waters just below the surface did not exist. Yet she was conscious all the time of their existence. How could she not be?

It was why she had to keep Luca at bay. She knew why she was doing it. To protect herself.

Not from his anger, as she had once said to him. But from something that was even more hurtful, even more wounding.

She heard his words to her that breakfast-time a month ago, carved into her.

'We can never be close.'

She led him upstairs, showing him the bedrooms, where the outdated wallpaper was gone, the patterned carpets replaced.

He would have brought Mia here. She'd have slept in the master bedroom, overlooking the lake she feared.

She put the thought from her.

'Which bedroom would you like for yourself?'

Luca's words penetrated, but she was confused. 'Me?' she said.

She would not be living here. She would be long gone. Living abroad was impossible now, Luca had made that clear, but she would settle somewhere on her own in Italy. Northern Italy…maybe Padua or Verona…so he could not accuse her of taking herself off too far. She hadn't thought about it much. Maybe she should start doing so.

He was glancing into another one of the bedrooms, filled with late-autumn sunshine, its walls a soft peachy tone, the carpet soft and deep. 'This would suit you,' he said, turning back to her.

She made no reply to that, saying instead that he should see the main bathroom, now comprehensively updated.

There were a couple of steps from the landing down to it, and in her hurry she caught her flat heel on one of them. Immediately a hand closed around her arm, steadying her.

'Are you all right?' There was concern in Luca's voice.

'I'm fine,' she said. She shook his arm off and headed into the bathroom, showing off its new splendour. He looked around him, but there was a faint frown on his face.

'You've been working very hard,' he said.

'Hardly,' she said. 'The work has all been done by others!'

'That's not what I meant. You've accomplished a great deal in a short time.'

She gave a shrug. 'Well, I need to keep busy. Just like you said.'

He looked down at her. She was conscious, without her high heels, of how petite she was against him.

'But now you need to slow down,' he said. 'You're coming up to your second trimester, when your scan will be due.'

'I'm pregnant, not an invalid,' she said briskly.

He put his hand out to her again, taking her arm. 'Ariana—'

'I'm fine,' she said. 'Don't fuss!'

She shook his hand off. She couldn't bear him touching her. Couldn't bear his concern.

It's for the baby—just for the baby... Not me. Never me.

Those words he'd thrown at her were still audible in her head.

'You're the last woman on earth I would want to marry.'

She silenced them. What else could she do except what she was doing now.

'There's more to show you,' she said, keeping her voice brisk.

For a moment he didn't move, just looked down at her, his face unreadable. She stepped past him, avoiding body contact, and went downstairs to the drawing room, opening the glass doors to the terrace. It was chilly outside, even in the sunshine. Winter was coming.

I must be gone by then.

'I've had the terrace by the lake-edge repaved, as we discussed,' she went on in her brisk, professional voice, 'and the stone balustrade strengthened for safety reasons. There's been quite a lot of pruning done, but it will be best to wait and see next spring and summer what the garden has to offer as it is.'

Luca stepped out beside her, looking around him.

'It will be good, come the spring,' he said, nodding. He looked down at her. 'And in the summer, with the baby…' something changed in his face '…it will be ideal for you.'

She said nothing, moving to turn away instead. But her hand was caught. She tried to draw it back, but Luca would not let go.

'Ariana…'

His voice was different again. He spoke in the way he'd said her name upstairs, when he was fussing over her. He caught her other hand, holding them both together in his so that she had to turn towards him. She tugged to free them.

A frown formed on his brow. 'You pull away from me all the time,' he said. 'But I only want to reassure you—'

'I don't want you touching me!' The words broke from her. Sharp. Insistent. 'It was you who said it, Luca—that we should be civilised. But there's too much…too much anger…hatred…for there to be anything else.' She looked at him, unflinching now. 'You said it yourself—we can never be close.'

She saw his expression change. 'I should not have said that.'

'Why not? It's true.' She took a breath. Felt emotion building in her. Finding its way to the surface. 'I know, Luca, that any concern you have is not for me. It is for the baby. I know it—and I understand it. I know that if I hadn't got pregnant I would never have set eyes on you again. I'd have let you take my business from me as punishment for what I did to you and gone off to starve in a gutter. And I would have been glad to do so if it got you out of my life! I curse the night I met you in New York! Curse that I ever let myself have anything to do with you! But now I have to. Because, as you said, we have to think not of ourselves and what we want—which for my part is to run like hell as far away from you as my legs will carry me!—but what this poor, poor baby is going to need…'

Her hand closed instinctively, protectively over her abdomen, which was starting to round now, to betray the presence of the living being within, who alone in all this mess was innocent of everything.

She would not cry, would not weep, even though she was cracking up inside, breaking into pieces. Numbly, she walked back inside, letting her torn and ragged emotions slowly subside, gaining mastery over herself again.

Indoors, she turned. He was standing in the open doorway to the terrace, looking at her, a troubled expression on his face.

She lifted her chin, squaring her shoulders. 'I've shown you everything,' she said, 'and now I'm hungry. Can we go and get lunch?'

Her voice was back to normal. The 'normal' she presented him with. The normal of being neutral and civil and civilised. The normal that had nothing to do with passion and hatred and destruction. Let alone anything else…

What cannot exist between us—what never will...

She walked out to his car, which was pulled up on the driveway, leaving him to lock up. Then waited for him to join her, staring at nothing.

Luca secured the villa's front door with Ariana's words echoing in his head. Rearranging things inside it. Though how, he did not know. He knew only that…

That I didn't want to hear them.

His frown deepened. Hearing that sharp, repudiating rejection—*I don't want you touching me!*—had circled like a shark biting. It was *he* who did not want anything to do with *her.* He who had walked away from her that morning in New York. He who had told her, that ugly night in Lucca, that he would never sully himself on her again. He who had said they could never be close. That any 'us' was only because of the baby.

He heard her words: *'I curse the night I met you.'*

They bit into him, but why should they? He was the one with regrets over that night.

Because I was already committed to Mia.

His eyes went to Ariana as he walked slowly towards the car, his thoughts rearranging themselves in his head, a frown still on his face.

What if Mia had not been in my life then?

He stopped. Motionless. What if he'd been free in New York? Free to stay with Ariana after their night together—their searing, unforgettable night?

I didn't want to want her.

His expression darkened. No, he hadn't wanted to want Ariana—and he still didn't want to want her.

Not because of Mia—Mia, he knew, with a kind of haunting sadness, was gone from him for ever, faded back into his boyhood dreams of what the ideal woman should be like.

Did she ever really exist for me or did I just invent her for myself? Place upon her all that I thought I yearned for in my ideal woman. Did I ever know her?

She had spoken so little, given away so little of herself—he hadn't even known she would have hated the villa by the lake…

Did I just conjure her from my dreams?

He tried to think now of what it would be like if it were Mia standing by his car—but he could not see her. She had gone…slipped away…a dream, a ghost…

Mia…sweet, gentle Mia…who had not deserved the treatment her own cousin had so humiliatingly and so viciously subjected her to at her wedding. Cruel and heartless—jealous and vindictive.

His expression steeled.

That was why he didn't want to want the woman he was going to have to marry now! The woman carrying his child. That was what he must remember—that hideous scene in the church and only that! Not Ariana telling him she could not take any more anger from him, with her tears falling on his hand, nor Ariana just now, pulling away from him, not able to bear him to touch her even when he meant her no harm…

He felt confusion well up in him…emotions dark and difficult deep within. They were making no sense.

He made himself start walking towards the car again. She was standing by the locked passenger door, staring into nothing. Her pregnancy barely showed under her loose top. A pregnancy she would never have told him about. If he hadn't discovered it she would have left Italy for ever.

I would never have seen her again.

He stopped dead.

That had been his intention that morning in New York as he'd left her there, lying in his bed. Never to see her again.

And if he hadn't—if he'd never set eyes on her again for the rest of his life…?

If that had been the reality, instead of this reality now…?

What would I feel?

He forced himself to close the distance between them. While inside his head all that he had been sure of was no longer there. Rearranged completely. But into what, he did not know.

* * *

Luca slowed to take a bend on the winding lakeside road, hemmed in between the plunging mountain slope to one side and the deep lake on the other, then accelerated again. His thoughts were inward, circling, as if he were an eagle high overhead, making no landing.

At his side, Ariana was studying her phone, looking at an invoice of some kind that she was scrolling through. Something to do with the villa refurbishment, he assumed.

His hands tightened on the wheel. He was not looking forward to the afternoon and what it would bring, but it had to be faced. It was all arranged.

She was closing her phone, slipping it back into her handbag. 'Where are we having lunch? Not too far, I hope. The electrician's turning up at three to put some more sockets in the utility room.'

Her tone of voice was as normal as it ever was when she was talking to him about the villa. But as he answered her he knew his voice was edged with tension. He would have preferred telling her over lunch, but she might as well know now. He had kept the preparations from her—it would be easier that way. It was something to be got through with as little fuss as possible—a mere legality for the sake of the baby they unwillingly shared, meaning nothing more than that. For either of them.

That was what he permitted himself to think about—not the questions circling in his head.

'You'll need to cancel him,' he told her. 'We won't be back by three.'

She turned to him, clearly about to say something,

but he did not let her. He made himself say what needed to be said.

'We're going to Como, Ariana. We're getting married—it's all arranged. Just a civil ceremony, obviously, simply to get it done.'

He'd kept his voice neutral, inexpressive, as he made the announcement, but at his side he heard her gasp.

'Are you *mad*?'

He set his face, not looking at her, only at the twisting road ahead. 'It has to happen, Ariana. I made that clear from the outset.'

He didn't want an issue made out of it. He'd undertaken to complete the paperwork, assembled the documents, made the necessary appointment as methodically as if he were preparing a business dossier. Now they just had to show up for the occasion itself. As brief and as businesslike as he could make it. Then it would be done.

She swivelled in her seat. 'And *I* made it clear that no way was I going to *marry* you!'

He could hear the protest in her voice. He slammed down on it—hard. Slammed down on the biting emotion starting to rise up in him at her protest.

'We will marry for the sake of the baby, to regularise its existence. As I said, it's all arranged, I've seen to all the paperwork. You just need to show up, that's all.' He felt his teeth gritting. 'Ariana, this has to happen! You know it as well as I do.'

'Luca—no! No, it does *not* have to happen! And it won't.'

'It *must*. Don't make me keep repeating myself!' Against his will he could feel his own tension rising.

'There's no "must" about it! It's totally unnecessary!'

'Ariana—' There was warning in his voice.

In hers, there was grim objection. 'I'm not marrying you! Luca, listen to me—'

'There is nothing for you to say! So don't waste your breath saying it!' His voice was harsh, impatient. He wanted her to stop protesting, objecting—arguing. There was nothing to argue about—no alternative to what had to happen.

But she was insisting on speaking. Protesting, objecting—arguing. The way his mother always had…

'Luca, *listen*, damn you! I am not marrying you! I am not marrying you now or ever! *Ever!* Do you hear me? *Ever!*'

Her voice was rising. He could hear anger in it… felt anger rising in him as well. This was not what he needed—not now! He heard his own words again—*It has to happen*—he didn't want her arguing about it, making difficulties, making a scene.

Out of nowhere, memory flashed. Decades old. A car journey with his parents, himself in the back seat, his father fuming in the driving seat, his mother sulking beside him. Angry about something. Taking it out on his father, sniping at him with her vicious tongue. His father's face darkening as he refused to rise to it. The building tension like a cloud in a thunderstorm. His mother's fury breaking…her shouting at his father, angry and denouncing.

He'd put his hands over his ears, but it hadn't blocked her out.

He slammed the memory shut.

'Enough!' The harshness in his voice was rough, angry. 'This is going to happen, Ariana—it's not open for debate!'

He would not look at her, would not listen. Unconsciously, he accelerated—as if to get to the wedding he didn't want but had no choice about even faster.

'I said *listen* to me.' Fury was boiling in her voice, along with frustration and protest.

The yank on the sleeve of his suit jacket, took him by surprise and his head whipped around.

'I am not marrying you!'

Her words were vehement, her face contorted, her fingers digging into his sleeve. Angrily, he shook his arm, dislodging her grip, and accelerated again, his face set, jaw clenched. Not bothering to speak because he'd already given her his answer. The only answer that was possible. Deny it all she wanted.

'Do you hear me, Luca? *Listen* to me!'

The yank on his sleeve came again, and this time his movement to dislodge her was more violent. He let go of the steering wheel with one hand to shake her off. With only his left hand steering his grip on the wheel was skewed. The imbalance made the tyres screech, the powerful car swerve, and he swore.

'Ariana—*stop*!' His head whipped around again, and fury was blazing in him now, as he felt her grab at his sleeve once more.

His eyes flashed forward. A tunnel was coming up—one of many along this winding, narrow lakeside road set between sheer mountain and deep lake. She was still gripping his jacket sleeve, dragging at his arm, and he gave it another violent shake to get rid of it. She was distorting his steering. He felt the tyres screech again.

'You can't make me marry you! I won't! *I won't!*'

Her cry was vehement, but he ignored it. Ignored the dragging grip on his sleeve…pulled at the steering wheel sharply as he felt the powerful, speeding car move diagonally—dangerously—across the carriageway. Urgently, he twisted the wheel to compensate, to get back to his own side of the road.

But not in time. A lorry, headlights blazing, was emerging from the approaching tunnel.

He did not even have time to swear before the crash came.

Ariana's eyes were opening and closing, making sense of nothing. Lights, far too bright. Voices, far too loud. Her hands were flailing uselessly as the trolley she was strapped on was rushed forward. She tried to speak but could not. No one was paying attention to her. Only to each other.

She could hear words, medical terms, spoken urgently, orders given. She tried to move, but her head was immobilised in some kind of padded frame. Then the trolley was moving again, through doors swinging wide, and she could see the rounded arch of a CT scanner ahead of her. Alarm filled her and she tried to speak again.

She must not have a CT scan, it would be dangerous for her baby—she had to tell them.

And where was Luca? Where *was* he?

She tried to say his name, but that was hopeless too.

The medics were sliding her into the scanner and she was told to stay still, quite still. It took only moments, and then she was being slid out again. A doctor was leaning over her. He was smiling.

'Your guardian angel was looking after you—and the car's air bags. There are no breakages, no internal injuries, only bruising and some lacerations. You'll be fine.'

He seemed about to rush off, but she made her hand snatch at him.

'My baby!' She forced the words from her throat, and this time they came out. 'Is my baby safe? I'm twelve weeks pregnant!'

The smile vanished from the doctor's face.

'Baby?' he said.

The doctor had given her painkillers to make her more comfortable, and they were keeping her in for observation as a precaution. But they would not say anything about Luca. Finally it was a nurse who told her, succumbing to her desperate pleading.

And when she did, the nightmare was complete.

'His legs took the full force of the impact. They were badly crushed. Surgery has stabilised him, but he will need much more.' The nurse paused, looking down at Ariana, her face strained. 'The surgeons will do everything they can, but…' she took a difficult breath '…it may be that they cannot save his legs.'

Horror drenched through Ariana—and a guilt so brutal she could not breathe.

She shut her eyes, as if that might stop the nightmare.

But nothing could do that.

* * *

Luca lay half propped up by his nurse against the pillows in his hospital bed. He'd been transferred to a hospital that specialised in orthopaedics. His rehabilitation had started, and soon the physiotherapist would be there to help him up…get him walking again on these strange, alien limbs.

But to what purpose?

He stared across the room. He had been here for weeks now, and it was as familiar to him as his own apartment. But he would be out of here as soon as he was able.

And then what?

He felt himself tense. As if he was guarding himself from the threat that was seeping into the room like a dark miasma.

He knew the name of it. Knew its power. Knew what gave it its power.

And it was not just the crutches leaning against the wall by his bed…

In his head, the words incised there by the letter left for him tolled with heavy blows.

He closed his eyes as if he could shut them out. Shut out both the words and who had written them. But nothing could. Nor ever would.

A soft knock on the door made him open his eyes again, unwillingly. A young nurse put her head cautiously around the door, not quite looking at him, and Luca knew why. Whatever appeal he had once held for her sex was impossible to detect any longer. His eyes were sunken, cheeks gaunt, face haggard.

As for the rest of him…

His mouth twisted.

'I know your physio is due, Signor Farnese,' the nurse began, sounding diffident, 'but you have a visitor who is very insistent on seeing you. She has come some distance, she says, and very much hopes you will agree to see her, however briefly.'

He froze. An emotion he would give no name to stabbed in his guts. Every muscle that still worked tensed like drawn wire. Slowly, he gave a curt, brief nod.

He steeled himself, his face a deliberate mask, as he fixed his gaze on the open doorway.

But the woman who walked through it hesitantly, uncertainly, was not the woman he'd thought it must be.

Shock went through him.

It was Mia.

CHAPTER THIRTEEN

ARIANA WAS SITTING on the narrow deck of the beach-front cottage, gazing out over the sugar-white sand that edged the flat sea beyond. She had been as touched as she'd been surprised when her mother had offered her this haven in Florida. But she was glad her mother was not actually at the grand villa behind the cottage, but was off skiing in Colorado.

She did not want to hear her mother say again, as she had on the phone, *'I know it's hard, but one day you'll be glad—'*

Ariana silenced her mother's voice in her head.

Glad?

Another voice came. The doctor at the hospital in Italy. Explaining, carefully—sensitively—what had happened.

Ariana had wept. Sobbed with a sense of heartbreak that had racked her body. The doctor had been kind, the nurses had been kind, everyone had been kind…

Yet still the sobs had come.

And a sense of bitter, bitter irony lacerated with a guilt so profound it had shaken her hand as she'd forced herself to write the letter she'd had to write. Guilt that would be with her to her dying day.

I caused it—I caused the crash. I and I alone.

Like red-hot skewers twisting into her, the self-blame came over and over again.

She shifted restlessly on her lounger.

I have to leave. I can't stay here for ever.

But where would she go and what would she do? Her business had been closed down—her accountant was winding it up. And as for going to London…there was no point now. Unconsciously, her hand splayed over her midriff. There was an ache inside her that could never be assuaged, shot through with guilt, regret and remorse…

She gazed blankly at the wintry sun reddening into a ball over the sea. Out on the beach a dog barked. Then another noise became audible. A motor of some kind… an electric hum.

She looked around. A wooden boardwalk ran down to the beach from the cottage and a motorised wheelchair was making its way along it.

Steering it was Luca.

He could see her. And he knew she had seen him. She had twisted her head around to stare at him, shock moving across her face. More than shock. Worse than shock.

Grimly, he powered on. The wooden boards were not ideal for the wheels of his chair, and the jolting, even though it was mild, sent pain shooting through him. He ignored the pain—it had become his habit to ignore pain.

He slewed onto the deck where she was sitting, still frozen, immobile, her knuckles white.

The woman he had thought never to see again.

But now he must.

Ariana felt the blood draining from her face. For a moment faintness whirled, then cleared. She jolted to her feet.

'What...what are you doing here?'

Her voice was a croak. The banal question she had uttered seemed so inadequate she could not believe she had asked it.

Did anything move in his eyes? There was no expression in his face, but that was not what she was looking at. What she was seeing was the greyness of it, the deep lines scored around his mouth—lines of pain. She felt emotion convulse inside her, seeing him looking the way he did. And another emotion too, that responded to it and made her pulse suddenly surge, countering the draining of blood from her own face.

But she must not feel that she mustn't.

The mask over his grey lined face did not move.

'I've come to talk to you,' he said.

She stared at him, still not believing that it was Luca here, now, on a winter beach in Florida. She saw his hands tighten, one resting on the arm of the wheelchair, the other on the control panel. His arms, his torso, moulded by the sweater he was wearing, looked as strong, as muscled as ever. Involuntarily, her eyes dropped to his lower body. Long trousers covered his legs...

Her stomach clenched with horror—the same horror

that had convulsed her when the nurse at the hospital had made that nightmare revelation to her.

He was speaking again. 'I've only just been released from hospital…' he took a sharp, harsh breath '…you left me a letter. I—'

She cut across him, voice twisted. Anguished. 'I had to tell you myself—not just leave it to the doctors!'

Something flashed across his gaunt face. 'I know,' he said. 'I understand.'

There was emotion in his voice now…emotion she did not want to hear. For it was the same emotion that was in her—one that could not be assuaged.

'But what I do *not* understand—' He broke off. Took another harsh, heavy breath, pinioning her with his gaze. As dark as obsidian…as searing as it had ever been…

Another emotion knifed through her—an old one… so old. And that, too, could never be assuaged…

He spoke again. His voice flat. 'Before I left the hospital I had a visitor,' he said. His eyes were behind that mask now. He paused, then said, 'Your cousin.'

'Mia?' Disbelief was naked in Ariana's voice. More than disbelief.

He gave a brief nod. 'She came to tell me some things.' His mouth compressed, and the expression in his eyes changed. 'Things you never thought to tell me.'

She swallowed. Unable to speak.

Luca's hand slammed down on the arm of his wheelchair. '*Why?* Why did you not tell me? Tell me that it was Mia who begged you to stop the wedding!' His voice was scathing. 'Because *she* didn't have the guts to do so herself!'

'That's not fair!' Ariana's defence of her cousin was automatic, immediate. 'Mia was distraught—'

'*Distraught?* She gave no sign of it! Do you understand me? Not one sign!'

Ariana shut her eyes, then opened them again. 'Mia's always hidden her feelings.' She swallowed. 'It's her way of coping with…with difficult situations…'

Luca stared at her. 'Coping with *what*, precisely? Being her grandfather's darling? What the hell was ever "difficult" about that?'

Ariana's face worked. 'You don't understand. Our grandfather smothered her…suffocated her. She was his favoured grandchild, but only if she was exactly the kind of grandchild he wanted her to be. She could never say no to what he wanted. Including…' her voice dropped low '…accepting your proposal of marriage. Because she knew,' she said sadly, 'it would make our grandfather happy. Then…then she felt trapped by it.'

'So she got you to do her dirty work for her and get her out of it. And you took the fall for it.' His voice was condemning.

Ariana swallowed. A sense of unreality was sweeping over her…to see Luca again…

She tried to focus, to keep only to listening to what he was saying. 'I had to find a way to stop the wedding without our grandfather realising Mia had never wanted to marry you. So that he would blame me instead.'

Luca's eyes were on her. It seemed unbearable to her that they should be.

'But it was not only your grandfather who blamed you, was it?' His voice was just as harsh, just as heavy.

'Not just he who accused you of acting out of vindictive jealousy.'

She looked away, giving a shrug. In her chest her heart was thudding. Her throat was tightening.

'Why did you not tell me the truth? That Mia never wanted to marry me!'

She could hear his incomprehension—and more. But what 'more' she did not know. Her eyes went back to him. She could see a nerve working in his cheek, haggard though it was.

'I… I didn't want your anger targeting her,' she said. She swallowed again. 'I knew I could take your anger, Luca. I've taken my grandfather's, so I could take yours. I'm strong—not like Mia. I wanted to protect her.'

'So you let me destroy you,' he said slowly. 'Blame *you*. Accuse *you*.'

She gave another shrug. It seemed so long ago now, in another life. What did it matter any longer? How could it when…?

'Oh, God, Luca—I'm so desperately, desperately sorry!' The words broke from her, and then her voice dropped, became intense and sombre. 'The guilt will be with me to my dying day. I caused that crash—it was my fault! And when the nurse told me—'

She turned away, unable to bear seeing him. Her breathing was ragged as she wrapped her arms around herself.

There was a sound behind her, but the blood drumming in her ears deafened her to it. And then, as she stood there, shaking with the horror of what she had done to him, hating herself more than it was possible to measure, she heard him say her name.

She turned back towards him. He was no longer in his wheelchair, but standing upright. Her thoughts flew in confused disarray—then they made sense.

Cold went through her—an icy flood through her body.

Prostheses. That was how he was standing there. Prostheses covered by his trousers so you could never tell their presence.

Had she said the word aloud? She didn't know. Only knew the horror of his damaged body that *she* had caused.

His expression was changing again. She saw him take a breath.

'Is that what you thought?' he asked.

There was something strange in his voice now.

Her mouth was dry. 'The nurse said…said the surgeons might not be able…able to save your legs…'

He was silent for a moment, standing there. So tall, so upright.

Memory seared through her—his long, lean body covering hers, their thighs meshed in that unholy passion that had fused their bodies but nothing else…

He was speaking, and memory vanished.

'Well, as you see,' he was saying, and his opaque gaze was holding her horror-struck one, 'the surgeons were, after all, very good at their job…'

A choke cracked in her throat, but he was still speaking.

'OK, I'm still very weak, and I still need physio, so

I use the chair for the time being, and there's enough metal in my legs to set off every airport security alarm I walk through. But *walk* is what I can do—and on legs that are mine. Still miraculously mine.'

Her hands flew to her mouth and that choking in her throat was now a sob, rising up unstoppably. Another followed it, and another, and then she could not stop them, choking and sobbing, pressing her hands against her mouth.

'Thank God—oh, thank God!'

Gratitude and thankfulness poured through her. He had been spared the ordeal she had so feared. Tears were pouring down her face now. Tears for so much. Tears not for relief, or gratitude or thankfulness. Tears of grief—tearing, unassuageable grief. For what had not been spared…

She felt arms come around her. Arms to hold her, to staunch her loss. *Their* loss. The arms of a man who had never held her as he held her now. To comfort her in her distress—in her grief at the loss of what she had once never wanted and now could only weep for. Such bitter, bitter tears…

She heard in her head the doctor's voice—kindly, sympathetic…pitying. And saw herself, not wanting to hear.

'It was not the crash. A silent miscarriage—that is what it's called. The body registers pregnancy, pregnancy hormones remain, the body prepares for birth, but no embryo is developing—the body has reabsorbed it. You would have been told so at your first scan.'

She had wept then, as she wept now, for the tiny life

that had had so short, so fragile an existence. For the loss she had had to tell Luca about in that stark, pitiful letter she had left for him.

Lucas's voice when he spoke was sombre. Strained. Filled with grief. Grief as deep as hers. 'Such a little life, and yet—'

He broke off, but she had heard the sorrow straining his voice.

She lifted her tear-stained face and when she spoke her voice was still choked. 'It seems so cruel! For our baby to have slipped away and we did not know…' She took a razored breath, making herself say what must be said. 'So cruel that I caused the crash that maimed and disabled you when we were driving to a wedding for which there was no reason.'

Her voice dulled and she pulled away. For he had no reason to hold her—none—and she had no claim on him, nor ever had.

'There was no reason, had we but known it, for you to have had anything to do with me.' Slowly, she shook her head. 'You're free of me, Luca—as I said at the end of my letter. That does not lessen my guilt about your injuries, though,' she said heavily. 'And all I can do is wish you a good recovery—'

She broke off, then made herself look at him. What did it matter now, with their baby gone, its fleeting existence snuffed out, whether he still thought her to blame for what she had done to stop his wedding to Mia? Guilty or innocent, it no longer mattered.

She spoke carefully, with difficulty. 'I'm… I'm sorry

your hopes of Mia were dashed—I know she's the one you wanted. Have always wanted.'

He was standing motionless, stiff-legged, and the strain in his gaunt face was visible. She felt emotion knife in her, but made herself go on.

'I've known since that morning in New York, Luca, that I was nothing but passing sex for you. A mistake, just as you said it was. Regretted the moment you awoke.'

Ariana saw his expression change, the acknowledging nod of his head, and though there was no reason for it that she would allow, it was like a knife twisting in an unhealable wound.

'Yes,' he said. 'Regret has been my dominant emotion, I agree. Regret for a great deal. But most of all…' his dark, obsidian eyes rested on hers '…for my own blind stupidity.'

And mine! she wanted to cry—but what would be the purpose? Everything between her and Luca had been a mistake. Causing nothing but misery and the loss of an innocent life that should never have existed, and so very nearly maiming a man to whom she had been, and always would be, nothing.

She heard his words in her head, still twisting that knife in her side. *'We can never be close—you are the last woman I would ever want to marry.'*

He was speaking again, his voice cutting across her bleak and painful thoughts.

'Blind stupidity,' she heard him repeat. 'The blind and unforgivable stupidity of my denial of what has been there from the very first.'

His eyes were on her, opaque, unreadable, yet there

was something in them that held hers to them as unbreakably as steel.

'My desire for you.' He drew a breath, harsh and heavy. 'A desire, Ariana, that I forced myself to deny from the moment I realised its overwhelming power.'

Her face contorted. 'And I know you hated yourself for it! You didn't want to want me! You said that to me! God, Luca, I know that—I know I meant nothing to you!'

'Because I would allow nothing else!' His voice slashed across hers and he took a breath, a shuddering one, that heaved in his chest as he exhaled again. 'Ariana, *why* do you think I walked out on you that morning in New York? If I'd stayed with you I would have been lost—'

He shifted position, a flicker of pain showing in his face as he did so. Abruptly, he spoke again. His voice was different now. Edged and guarded.

'Do you never wonder what made me want to marry Mia? Quiet and gentle and sweet and passionless.'

His expression changed again. There was a distant look in his eyes now, and they were shifting again, a bleakness in them.

'Because that was what I valued. Craved. To make a quiet, placid marriage! Totally unlike my own parents' marriage—' He broke off, his gaze turning inward. Then, 'Their marriage was hell. Thanks to my mother. She revelled in making scenes, raging at my hapless father, not caring what people thought, how they stared at her, shocked. She would make furious accusations, denunciations, storming at my father with her endless demands and complaints, and always, *always* my father tried to placate and appease her. He never, ever stood up to her—because he was besotted by her, abjectly in her thrall. And I *vowed* that I would never be like him! Never entrust myself to a woman who had any power over me.'

His voice hardened and his gaze opened to hers, returning to the present.

'Least of all sexual power.'

He drew a breath, harsh and heavy, his mouth compressing.

'And then I encountered you. And I found that my desire for you—which I could not resist that night in New York, though I knew...*knew*... I should—had the power to make me betray the quiet, gentle woman I had found in Italy, whom I had thought the ideal wife for me.'

His voice was condemning.

His face darkened.

'Everything you threw at me that morning...every accusation as I walked out on you...was true. And it burned like a brand on my skin that it should be so! I used that burn to tell myself how your rage and fury was the very proof of how impossible you were for me! How right I was to walk away...to go back to Mia thinking I would find the peace with her that I thought was what I craved.'

The expression in his eyes changed.

'It was the worst decision of my life.'

Ariana stood there, hearing him speak, unable to move a muscle. A pulse started to throb in her constricted throat. She saw Luca turn away, walk haltingly to his wheelchair, sink down in it. Pain flashed across his face as his legs bent, then relief as the pressure on them was lifted.

'Forgive me,' he said. 'I cannot stand for long yet.'

He lifted his face to look at her, and in his eyes was an openness she had never seen before. And his next words were an admission she had never heard before.

'Mia was a mirage, conjured out of my own fears. She was never real.' He looked away, out over the distant sea He paused, then spoke again with difficulty. 'I… I never knew her. Not the person she was. And…' he took a breath, also with difficulty '…and I nearly ruined her life as well.' He frowned, looking back at Ariana. 'I… I am glad she has found her own happy ending—her husband Matt was with her when she came to see me in the hospital. But as for me—' He broke off. Then, 'I should have stayed with you,' he said. 'I should have stayed, after our night together, and faced up to what had happened.'

His voice was harsh, and Ariana felt herself swallow, as painfully as if a stone were lodged there. 'We had sex, Luca, that was all.'

'No.' It was a blunt, one-word contradiction. 'That was not all.' He closed his eyes for a moment, then they flashed open again. 'You know it was not all, Ariana! You know that had I not walked out I would never have gone back to Italy to marry Mia. She would have become meaningless.'

And now his voice was different again, and his eyes fastened on hers with so dark a power she could not break it, so dark a power she could no longer breathe.

'Because since that night only one woman—only one!—has had any meaning for me at all.'

He drew in a breath, a rasp. His hands tightened on the arms of the wheelchair.

'You, Ariana. The woman I did not want to want. The woman I could no more *not* want, *not* desire, than I could not breathe, could not see or hear or taste! The woman who fills the world for me.'

'You said I was the last woman you would want...' Her voice was a whisper.

'I lied. I lied to save my own sorry skin. I lied to make the lie a truth. A truth that had died the first time I set eyes on you.' He shut his eyes for a moment, then opened them. 'Oh, God, Ariana, I have been the world's fool! You gave yourself to me in passion and in flame and I threw you away! I lied to myself, and to you, over and over again. Told myself I was glad—dear God—*glad* that you had proved my fears of you right, that you had acted out of jealous rage at your innocent cousin!' His voice changed. 'I told myself that the only reason I took you to Milan was because of the baby. That that was the only reason we were together.'

'But there is no baby, Luca. Not any more.' Her voice was sad.

She looked out to sea. The sun was setting now in a golden orb. Memory came of how she had stood watching the sun over Lake Como when Luca had first taken her to the villa. It seemed a lifetime ago.

'No. But there is us, Ariana.'

Her gaze came back to him. He was looking at her

with something in his face she had never seen before, something that stopped the breath in her lungs.

His voice as he spoke again was low and strained. 'I've screwed up with you from the very first to the very last,' he said. 'I have neither hope nor expectation.' His mouth twisted in a simulacrum of bitter humour. 'I haven't even a sound body to offer you.' Something changed in his eyes. 'And yet all the same whatever I have, I offer you, Ariana. If any of it should by any chance be of any use or worth or value to you, then it is yours.'

She looked at him as if she had never seen him before. Because the man she saw now had never existed before. The man within the man. The man who had, in a single moment, said the most precious words to her. Precious beyond all measure—because she had never hoped for them. Never dared to hope for them.

Emotion welled within her, rising like a tide long stopped, long held at bay. Now no longer.

'There is us.'

She felt her throat constrict…her heart crushed within her. The world stopped. She walked up to him, reached out her hand. But not to take his.

'There is only one part of you that is of any use or worth or value to me,' she said. 'And it is this.'

Slowly, carefully, she placed her hand on his chest, where the beat of his heart could be felt. And she felt it now, strong and quickening. Felt his hand lift from the arm of the wheelchair, flash out and close around hers. Her legs buckled and she went down on her knees on the deck, her other hand lifting to his face, cupping his haggard cheek, then dropping away.

Words came, halting and painful, confessing and self-castigating. 'You kept rejecting me, Luca. Always rejecting me! From that first hideous morning in New York, after the most incredible night of my life. You had swept me off my feet and into your bed, to fall asleep in your arms and dream that in the morning would begin the greatest romance of my life, with a man who was like no other in the world, the one man for me! And then—' Her voice cracked. 'To wake and realise you were gone…just gone. You walked out on me, discarded me. And then—oh, God—worse still was what you threw at me. That you had slept with me *knowing* you were going back to Italy to marry…'

The words were choking her, but she had to say them—*had* to. Because they were gutting her, eviscerating her…

'And after I stopped your wedding that hatred in you for me, that deadly rage… You did all that you could to have your revenge on me, to destroy me. And you did. And then that nightmare night in Lucca, when I wanted to hit back at you in the only way I could, to reject *you* as you had rejected me…but I couldn't… I just couldn't—'

His voice cut across hers. Harsh—but not at her. Never harsh at her any more. 'Nor could I reject you—though I loathed myself for my weakness!'

She gave a cry that was half a sob, felt tears starting to burn in the backs of her eyes. 'And you loathed me, too! And you went on and on rejecting me—even when you were forcing yourself to marry me you were telling me that I was the last woman on earth you would ever want! Always rejecting me—*always*!'

She bowed her head.

'And I didn't know why it hurt so much! I'd been rejected so often in my life—by my mother, my father, my grandfather. I was used to it! Your rejection should not have hurt me as it did—so why did it? *Why?*'

She screwed her eyes shut so tight the tears on her lashes scalded her cheeks.

'I've faced it now—faced what I never wanted to face! That you could only hurt me, Luca, because...' she swallowed, and it was agony to do so '...because I loved you.' Her voice dropped. 'Though I cursed myself for it.'

'And you cursed the day you met me.' Luca's voice was heavy. He took a ragged breath, his hand tightening on hers. 'When you said that to me it was like a knife going into me—though I did not know why. Not then. But now—'

He broke off. Took her other hand, curled defensively in her lap, folded them within his, protectively...cherishingly. She heard the catch in his voice as he spoke again.

'Be mine. Be mine, Ariana of my heart. As I am yours, loving you as I now know I do—fool that I have been. Be mine as I am yours. Be *mine*.' His voice was choked now, and her tears flowed faster yet. 'And when we conceive in love and joy, in passion and desire, the child *will* come—for the sake of the baby we lost...'

She clutched his hands more tightly, her face uplifted to his. 'It seemed such a dreadful sign,' she said, weeping still for so much...for the child that had not been. 'It seemed like a sign of what had created it in the first place—a sign that it should never have existed, never *could* exist between us…so toxic, so poisoned…'

He silenced her—silenced her with a kiss so gentle it was like a breath of air, no more. A kiss such as had never been between them till now.

'We shall make right all that was wrong,' he said. 'It will be a second chance for us. And I promise, Ariana of my heart, with all my being, that I will never, ever bring hurt to you again—only all the love in my heart, for ever.'

She smiled at him mistily, tears brimming yet again. Her heart was overflowing with all that he had said. With all the wrongs that had been made right. It sang inside her, a paean to him.

'I ask only one promise of you,' she said. 'That you will never leave me.'

'Never,' he agreed.

He turned his head, looking about him. His gaze swept around from the beach, where the sea was pooling with the setting sun, turning to bronze, and the white sand was darkening to gold, back to the little wooden cottage. Dusk was gathering towards coming night.

'Could we start my never leaving you right now?' he asked, and there was something different in his voice which made her catch her breath, quickened the pulse at her throat.

She felt the wash of his eyes over her, a heat beating up in her as he brushed his mouth against hers and lifted her hand in his.

She straightened, getting to her feet, keeping hold of

his hand as he got to his feet too, their eyes never leaving each other, her hand tightening in his.

'Oh, Luca, man of my heart—yes…*yes*!'

His arms came instantly around her, folding her to him, and it was bliss, oh, such bliss, to be in his arms again. Bliss to lift her face to his and be kissed by him. Softly, tenderly, sweetly… And then with more than tenderness. So much more…

She led him indoors. Into the rest of her life. And his.

'I don't want to hurt you…' Ariana's voice was anxious.

'You can never hurt me. Not now that I know I am yours, and that you have forgiven me for what I did to you.'

Luca's voice in the dusk, in the dimness of the bedroom, as he lay beside her on the bed, was husky.

'But it could be that you make the moves,' he went on, smoothing the waterfall of her hair from her brow as she lifted her mouth from his, and she could hear the wry and rueful note in his low voice.

'Every one,' she promised him, her voice warm, and so, so loving.

And so she did make the moves, with gentle hands and fingertips that explored in glory the wonder of his body, that smoothed with a little cry of grief for the scars scored into his stricken legs. But he would not let her weep again for him. He would only let her move her body over his, carefully, slowly, to ensure that all she brought to him was pleasure and not pain.

Slowly, sensually, as the night darkened around them, she made love to him, took his body into hers. Bestowed herself upon him. Wound her arms around him, felt his arms around her, holding her close, so close…

The moment when they came together, with a soft, breaking cry from her, a low, helpless groan from him, their bodies were meshed and fused and melded together, so that parting was impossible. For they were made one flesh. One body. One being. One heart beating…

She wept again, knowing how long and terrible a journey it had been to this moment, knowing all that it had cost them both. Including the little life they had created, so pitifully lost to them…

Surely another little life would come? She hoped so with all her being, even as Luca, careless of his scars, his still wasted muscles, his bones knitted together with steel and the patient skill of surgeons, swept his body over hers so that it sheltered her, stroking her hair, cradling her to him, murmuring to her of all that was and always would be.

One love between them.

For all time.

EPILOGUE

CAREFULLY, ARIANA LOWERED herself into the padded chair on the semi-circular terrace outside the villa's drawing room. Beyond the gardens sunlight glittered on the lake's dark surface.

It was good to be out of the maternity hospital.

Good to be home again.

Home.

Though Luca still had his ferociously modernistic apartment in Milan, it was the lakeside villa that was home—and it was glorious. Spring was ripening into summer, and the gardens were lush with flowers and greenery. She felt emotion pluck at her. Had she really once thought she would never live here? That it was nothing to do with her?

Her eyes went to Luca, stepping through the open French windows, a precious bundle in his arms. The two people she loved most in all the world. Her heart turned over, and she felt love and happiness and thankfulness drenching through her.

'Here he is,' said Luca, carefully lowering their adored baby into her waiting arms. 'Wide awake again.'

His voice was tender, doting, and Ariana loved him all the more for it. Loved their son all the more, too, overcome by a wave of tenderness. She smiled, gazing as dotingly as Luca at the tiny infant wrapped in his cotton blanket, his starfish hands waving slowly, his little mouth mewing.

'And hungry again!' She laughed, slipping the buttons on her maternity blouse, feeling her milk come in.

He latched on hungrily, and for a while neither she nor Luca did anything but gaze in wonder and mutual adoration. And thankfulness. Such thankfulness.

Without volition, Ariana felt tears prick the back of her eyes. Luca saw them, and hunkered down beside her, taking her free hand as she cradled their nursing child.

'I like to think,' he said, his voice low with deep-felt emotion, and knowing why she had become tearful, 'that he is the baby we lost—this time come again safely and healthily.'

She pressed her fingers into his, gazing across at him, eyes misting. 'How blessed we are, Luca,' she said.

She looked about her at the gracious house she'd restored, the gardens lush all around them, the dramatic lake edged with the mountains beyond—and the man beside her whom she loved so, so much.

And he loved her. As she had never thought he could—or would. And yet he did.

He leant forward, kissing her softly. 'Blessed indeed,' he said, straightening, then sitting himself down opposite her, crossing one long leg over the other.

His legs had healed almost completely, and that was another cause for her profound gratitude. It was a gratitude that Luca had shown in a massive donation to the hospital whose surgeons' skills had saved his limbs, and to the orthopaedic centre where he'd regained the use of them.

And that was not the only use his money had been put to.

Ariana smiled fondly at him. 'Your investment in Matt's career continues to pay off—he and Mia are charting with their latest release, she tells me.' She paused a moment. 'She says she wants us to visit when she and Matt are next in Italy.'

Luca looked at her. 'I will do so gladly.' It was his turn to pause. 'Ariana, she was a dream, a mirage—unreal in herself to me. I wronged her almost as much as I wronged you.'

His voice was sombre, and Ariana hated to hear it.

'It's in the past, Luca—and both she and I have found our happiness!' Her expression changed. 'I still find it astonishing that it's turned out to be Mia who is the secret to Matt's success! That she has such a beautiful voice. And,' she went on, 'how wonderful it is that our grandfather is now reconciled to her!'

It was true. A penniless musician and an eloping granddaughter had turned into a commercially and artistically successful musical duo—one for Tomaso to be proud of and one who made sure they spent a lot of time in Italy with him at his *palazzo.*

And although Ariana knew wryly now, rather than bitterly, that her grandfather would never be proud of *her*, in having a granddaughter who had married Luca

Farnese—even if it was the wrong one!—he could not be as scathing of her as had once been.

'I think you'll find,' Luca was saying drily, 'that you too have gone up in his approval ratings by providing him with his first great-grandson…'

She gave a wry laugh. 'I doubt my poor mother will ever forgive me for turning her into a grandmother—however glamorous!'

'She'll love him when she sees him,' Luca promised her. 'As will your grandfather.'

On cue, their son unlatched, gazing up at them, then started to mewl again.

'Time for *dulce*,' Ariana said, and busied herself swapping him to her other side, conscious, with a little colour in her cheeks, of how Luca's eyelashes dipped down over his dark obsidian eyes as his gaze rested on her exposed breast. It would be a while yet before he could do more than look, but Ariana was already impatient…

She met his gaze as it returned to her face, remembering in vivid detail the passion that burned between them. For the moment it was only a memory—but soon…

'Don't look at me like that…' Luca's voice was husky. 'New fatherhood is miraculous, but it has its drawbacks…'

She laughed, tossing back her hair, cuddling her suckling infant closer to her breast. The necessary days would pass, her post-partum body would heal, and then… Oh, then…

Luca leant across to kiss her. Lightly and gently. With the promise of so much more to come.

The promise of eternal love and happiness for all their days together.

And all their nights…

Definitely all their nights.

* * * * *

Enchanted by
The Cost of Cinderella's Confession?

Then don't forget to check out these other magical stories by Julia James!

The Greek's Duty-Bound Royal Bride
The Greek's Penniless Cinderella
Cinderella in the Boss's Palazzo
Cinderella's Baby Confession
Destitute Until the Italian's Diamond

Available now!

COMING NEXT MONTH FROM

#4073 INNOCENT MAID FOR THE GREEK

by Sharon Kendrick

Self-made Theo watched his new wife, Mia, flee minutes after signing their marriage papers. Now Theo must persuade the hotel maid to pretend to reunite for the sake of her grandfather's health. But being so close to her again is sensual torture!

#4074 PREGNANT IN THE ITALIAN'S PALAZZO

The Greeks' Race to the Altar

by Amanda Cinelli

Weeks after their passionate encounter on his private jet, Nysio can't get fashion designer Aria out of his head. He's determined to finish what they started! Only, in his palazzo, they discover something truly life-changing—she's expecting his baby!

#4075 REVEALING HER BEST KEPT SECRET

by Heidi Rice

When writer Lacey is told to interview CEO Brandon, she can't believe he doesn't recognize her—at all...even if her life has dramatically changed since their night together. Then their past and present collide and Lacey must reveal her biggest secret: their child!

#4076 MARRIAGE BARGAIN WITH HER BRAZILIAN BOSS

Billion-Dollar Fairy Tales

by Tara Pammi

After admitting her forbidden feelings for her boss, Caio, coding genius Anushka is mortified! So when he proposes they marry to save their business, she's conflicted. Because surely his ring, even his scorching touch, can never be enough without his heart...

HPCNMRA1222

#4077 A VOW TO SET THE VIRGIN FREE

by Millie Adams

Innocent Athena has escaped years of imprisonment...only to find herself captive in Cameron's Scottish castle! His marriage demand is unexpected but tempting. Because being bound to Cameron could give Athena more freedom than she believed possible...

#4078 CINDERELLA HIRED FOR HIS REVENGE

by Emmy Grayson

Grant longs to exact vengeance on the woman who broke his heart. When Alexandra needs his signature on a business-saving contract, he finally gets his opportunity. This time, when their passion becomes irresistible, *Grant* will be the one in control!

#4079 FORBIDDEN UNTIL THEIR SNOWBOUND NIGHT

Weddings Worth Billions

by Melanie Milburne

Aerin needs cynical playboy Drake to accompany her to a glamorous event in Scotland. She knows her brother's best friend *isn't* Mr. Right. But when a snowstorm leaves them stranded, she can't ignore the way Drake sets her pulse racing...

#4080 THE PRINCE'S ROYAL WEDDING DEMAND

by Lorraine Hall

The day innocent Ilaria stood in for her cousin on a date, she didn't expect it to be at the royal altar! And when Prince Frediano realizes his mistake, he insists Ilaria play her part of princess to perfection...